THE
ROAD TO NEOZON
STORIES
ANNA TAMBOUR

THE
ROAD
TO
NEOZON

stories

ANNA TAMBOUR

OBSIDIAN SKY BOOKS

DETROIT, MI

THE ROAD TO NEOZON
Copyright © 2018 Anna Tambour

Obsidian Sky Books
Detroit, USA

ISBN: 978-1-7322980-0-2

Cover art and interior design by
Nathaniel Hébert, *www.winterhebert.com*

ALSO BY ANNA TAMBOUR

NOVELS
Smoke Paper Mirrors
Crandolin
Spotted Lily

COLLECTIONS
The Finest Ass in the Universe
Monterra's Deliciosa & Other Tales &

CONTENTS

to Ed Yeatman
who least expects it

A DROP IN THE OCEAN

HEY, don't toss your cigarette butt at me. And don't look around like you're someone else. I know your face. Musta seen it for what, thirty years? I got a memory like you wouldn't believe.

And look at me when I'm talking to you. The moon's not gonna help you. What you see in that big fat face? The moon buffs my tops. Never look up to someone on the same footing as you. They're no use. The moon's just a worker with no more pulling power, power where it counts—than you.

Unfair? Who's fault is it your taking shit from anyone? Especially from those old farts you're whining about who stink of diapers, booze, cover-up perfumes? And whose fault is it you hold onto your accent like it's some precious mineral?

That's no excuse. Look, there's no one who knows people better than me. Hey, you have NO IDEA how many I've known, and I don't like to think of myself as old, but I was around before you were a mistake in your daddy's pants, and I'm telling you—

So they mistake you. This is sad, so sad. The people are always right. You think I should sympathise? Sympathy is for losers.

That's a good one. You think I'd spend *my* life like some little mud wallow? I could make two continents and your birthplace swim with the fishes if I wanted. If I wanted. The moon gives me massages. Right now what, a billion, billion and a half people are admiring me or trying to get within sight of me. And it gets bigger every day, as I get bigger. The moon's poetry, man, while I'm everyone's obsession. Didn't they name a perfume Obsession? I could take out—

Hey, Whine and Grosses, it's rude to interrupt. Don't go! I can help you. I've helped a lot of people. So many people.

Even I can't change that. Trust me. If you talk like a duck you must be a duck even if your papers say you're a sword-fish. You're in a bad way. A very bad way. Like a sardine in a baitball.

No, I'm not saying you'll be snatched up, but my instincts tell me, and that adds up to that duck. I can feel it about you. And there's worse.

Your family? You shouldn't have had those children if you weren't prepared to work hard enough to succeed. You see me making do with lesser expectations of myself? No one could accuse *me* of being a sardine. Everyone in the world knows of me, but who are you? See what I mean?

Stop that. Crying is weak. You see me cry? Let's face facts. You must be already on a list and it's only time before they come for you, could be soon as the next tide.

It won't help, and you know it. Look, I'm very instinctual, can't you see? And so, so deep. You can feel it in your guts that I am right. That knock on the door—

I told you. People tell me things. It's just the way I am. I'm so approachable, you should know. If you didn't trust me, you wouldn't have told me how low you are. How you let them say things to you. I've got no spine but you don't see me putting up with—

Fat use 'I have to' has done you. I—no, you've already told me. And no, dogs are not treated better, so many dogs. But why are we still talking about you suffering? Believe in me and save yourself before—

Maybe when the ship lands. Maybe the night after, which would be MUCH worse. You don't want your wife,

Maria isn't it? Whatever, you don't want your woman and kids seeing you pee your pants. Disgusting.

Yes, I can see it. Nobody can predict like I can. Later, you'll meet lotsa people I've saved who will tell you that. So many people. Huge schools.

Yes, lawyers, too. And judges. And criminals like you. Yes, not like you but if you're gonna let your ego get in the way—

Innocence? That's no help. It's a weakness. You're soft as a rotting whale.

Help? You think anyone but me is gonna help you when you need it? Before you're some one minute too-late headline? When does that happen in real life, unless you're a winner?

Don't waste my slosh talking about your relatives, or groups. Intervention? You believe in that down here, you get chomped.

I was just saying. Don't *worry*. I'll protect you.

Rights? Don't make me laugh. You know no one who counts. Only I can fix you.

Look, I'm more patient than anyone else in the world, but you're taking up valuable time. I'll only say this once again. No one else has thought of your family as much as I have, of their needs, their quality of life. Their lives will be so, so beautiful, you can't imagine. You don't have the experience. But you must act now.

That's the best thing about it. You don't have to think it out. And there's nothing you need to study up about. That's my job. And I'm the best in the world with this kind of thing. I love you people. And now that we've looked at each other so much, you know in your heart that I know you better than you know yourself. That's okay. You don't have the capacity.

Here, wipe your face. You don't wanna look disgusting, do you? Good to see you finally helping yourself—it's going to be SO good! You'll—hey, where you going? Shit, no! What self-respecting body would write a note? You're done explaining. And you've wasted enough of my time.

I forgive you. Well said. You sure do have your limitations. Now let's do it. You're gonna love it. No one can take care of you like I.

Yes, I told you already. They'll be rolling in benefits, and you'll be a hero. Where else can you achieve these heights, that you don't even deserve, but I love you people. It's my weak spot, and—as I said, my instinct says about you that bad—

Thank you. I know you're grateful. So jump.

A leap of faith? Obviously. Jump.

No, I'm not in a bad mood, but you're liable to make me so. After all, who's ever heard of you? And who doesn't know me?

Come *on* already. You've got nothing left to lose. Jump and I'll catch you.

A picture-postcard sea, a perfectly selfie scene, the Carnival Cruises ship's wide butt trails a broad white wake, the moon at two o'clock working its buffing rays on the ocean's tops—the moon's fat depressed face looking as if wanting to say something, as if wanting to have said something, as if wishing it had intervened; wishing it could at least say sorry though what could it have done? The crinkle in the eyes is almost mean, as if it's wishing it could turn those shiny white blades down below—the tops of waves—into stabbing instruments, as if stabbing the water could make the ocean bleed. The moon fight the ocean and win? Preposterous hope. A fantasy for losers. And that face on the moon, like its capacity for emotion, its silly compassion: like all fairy tales—FAKE! The moon no more needs a face to do its work than it needs a voice.

In the depths of the ocean much stirs, including the disappearing rumble of the ship's bank of engines. In the tropical air above, the ship's ambient noise of Entertainment is a thinning slick.

Soon the air here only carries the sound of a light wind

such as you hear when you plug your ears, the odd sharp seabird cry—and as far as the ear can hear, the thuds of whitecaps clapping against each other.

And the moon? That worker is out as usual, on its endless round of tides.

Love, fear, and thankless work keep the world in order.

But also, there must be play.

Out beyond this horizon, the ocean's having a whale of a time catching a little family. Afterwards, the child's doll will be found, fulfilling its destiny as the closest thing this family will get to a black box, the doll will be seen making— if the right people see it—a human interest story. If not, it becomes another child's toy. A child who might one day, also be tempted by the ocean's patter.

And people, if the doll on the beach makes it into another human interest story, will cry and blame each other or a storm, same as they do when a church's destruction costs believers their lives so that other believers live to build another.

People die all the time in places they worship, same as they die all the time at sea—the blame sliding off gods and oceans easy as water off that proverbial duck's back. Though in people's love, there's desperate worry. Places of worship are built as fortresses. And even as the oceans are predicted to become so big, they take over land, people love them so much, they cluster near the very edges where the ocean is most likely to overcome the land. Yet "The Ocean's at Risk" scream the headlines. "The Oceans are Dying" is a truism. But oil can pour on the waters till the sea looks like marbled paper, and it's like a doctor jabbing a patient. It doesn't hurt the ocean, just those in it. Coral bleaching? That's the coral. Fish stocks plummeting? Fishermen and laws to blame there. But what's less fish to the sea? The ocean we've witnessed is, with its global network, the most powerful force today—and in its power, above blame. "I can do anything," it has said, and for once, it might be right.

A boat can capsize killing all it carried, and a storm is blamed. Fishermen die every day, plucked from boats, snatched from rocky shores, as some ocean bats them around till they die of exhaustion. Indeed, fishermen are like those rodents with infected brains, coming to be played with to death—but Fate or Bad Luck, the never-divorced spouses of losers are always blamed. But oceans can do anything. "I could drown the most loved person in the world and I wouldn't lose any lovers," this ocean brags to itself, quite truthfully. Just yesterday it promised one beautiful, romantic, heartbroken woman a bracelet with the moon as the charm. And she fell for it. To a child, the ocean rippled the moon's reflection, calling it a rubber ball to kick. Another drop in the ocean. The boy's shoe might be found some day.

Shores everywhere are littered with the oceans' castoffs, dragged there by the pull of the moon, who is unwilling but unable to stop.

The moon has seen so much by oceans everywhere, for they're all the same even though one is called 'pacific.' Mutely, the moon must watch but that doesn't mean it doesn't or can't reflect upon its memories.

As it works, maybe it mindfully looks back—back to when it worked with the tireless fanaticism of an artist of leisure.

Now, the moon has been around long enough to know that past performance doesn't guarantee future results, but the moon's seen many cycles. And time and time again, for times that each seemed crystallized, all that glittered was ice—ice, ice, everywhere. Endless drifts—walked on, hacked at, wind-chapped. Ice—tortured by the playfully cruel sun, moonshined by that old poker-faced perfectionist moon. Ice shrieking as it rubs against itself. Ice, stain-streaked from the shit of innumerable unmentionable things.

From sea to shining sea, every ocean—well locked up.

THE GODCHILDREN

T HE side-street was so narrow that the fashionable woman's left hip scraped a groove into the historic stone buildings while the poodle she was walking got a right-side shave.

"How'd you think they'll get down that?" said Nat. "We should leave. Meet them all somewhere else. *If* you know somewhere else. And you *better*."

Jet dug his spoon into his bowl, his cool making Nat tremble.

"This is the best ice cream anywhere," said Jet.

"As if you've had ice cream before."

"I've had ice cream," Jet lied, wishing Nat would just shut up. This ice cream was what living should be about. It was the brilliant red of Firstborn's fifth eye. Jet had never known food could taste. He'd picked this place because it seemed perfect—so opposite anything they'd ever known. Until they'd entered, it hadn't occurred to him to actually *imbibe* something, but he regarded himself as an adventurer, so he'd asked the old man who seemed to be the sole worker here, for one serving—the old man to decide what. The trays of choices all looked filled with cold slightly slimy ooze—nothing out of the ordinary to a lakebed in Massachusetts, but this mud was separated into colored versions of the primordia many of his siblings lived in. None of them ate it, but when in Rome... (not that he'd ever before been west or east of Mass).

With the first spoonful, Jet grew tastebuds… that flowered. He dug another spoonful out and as he held it in front of him, a factory set to work inside him, producing ols. He had heard of smell before, of course he had. Weren't he and all his siblings supposed to emit smells? Hadn't Father declared those emanances to be: stench? And wasn't stench loathsome? Yet another one of the hideosities that made Jet, Nat, and all his siblings, even Firstborn, objects to fear, hate, revile, and describe and classify in the most abjurant terms. Stench? He had never before *wanted* to be able to smell— all that shame he would feel when he sniffed his repellency. Not that he'd had the choice. Whether Father had genetically rigged his godchildren, Jet had speculated fruitlessly. Certainly every one of the siblings had not what you'd call the full Swiss-Army-knife set of anatomy, though many had quite specialized equipment.

Jet hadn't experienced smell before. This ice cream stuff was pure happiness. What would stench smell like? He supposed the opposite of this. He exercised his ols, yet could only smell things he wanted to roll in, he was so enjoyant.

Across the small round table, Nat was seething. He hadn't even tried the ice cream, had never to Jet's knowledge, put anything in his mouth.

"You trying to kill me?" he had said when Jet offered to order for him. "Just a touch of collagen, I break out in hands."

"Hands?"

"Don't act incredulous. Hands, all over me. And what's worse, each of them has… ugxh… *fingers!*"

Jet suppressed a retch at the image. He'd never known. "You want me to ask for collagen-free—?"

"Shut up and eat."

"But collagen? In ice cream?"

"You're so insensitive. Don't you realize the extra pain you put me through, to have to tell you?" Nat started mumbling to himself. Nat's nerves. He'd always been high-strung, paranoid, pessimistic. Funny that.

Amazing that all Father's offspring hadn't picked up his traits. Here they were, twins, yet Jet felt alive as never before. Almost as if "you can be anything you want" was really true and not a myth.

Whatever, without the cloud of hate and fear that blanketed him and all Father's godchildren back home, this island adventure was going to be a blast, no matter what the rest of the siblings turned out to be like. Jet raised his spoon without thinking, and the old man rushed forward with another bowlful, this time the purported color of Firstborn's teeth.

"Vanilla," he said to Jet. "We grow it here." His smile was so wide, you could count each of his four teeth and see all the way to the back of his shiny pink gums.

Jet tasted this new stuff, and glowed with happiness. He thanked the old man vociferously.

"What was that about?" said Nat. "You speak whatever they speak here?"

"But of courth," said Jet, his mouth partly frozen from all the ice cream in it. "Anyone who wants to can make themselves understood. But of course," he yelled, "You could have picked someplace better if you hadn't been too lazy."

"Shhh, Jet. You want to get us killed? Look where you've brought us. Outside of that oldie who would love anyone who eats his food, who do you see?"

Nat had a point. If this had been back home, it would be the proverbial lions' den. The place was packed, every little round table surrounded by (it was enough to melt your viscera) *young men*.

Young men. Nat had hardly been able to get in the door of this place, the sight had struck him so dumb and still with fear. And here Jet was acting as if young men weren't the very army stirred by the call of Father himself, the father who through some kind of genesis, had sired all by himself countless deities that he spoke of as if they'd been excreta.

Yes, their father whose art had made 'Nat,' 'Jet,' and all their kind, had so hated his offspring that he damned them soon as he had them, and tossed them out so that in their very homeland they would be forever loathed, supposedly feared, but definitely attacked in purported self-defense. It all made Nat boil.

"None of us have ever hurt a fly, not even a baby human." He gripped a fold of Jet. "And look at them, just waiting to attack."

"Yes, look," said Jet, pushing Nat down into the little chair so hard that Nat was embossed by iron filigree. He couldn't move, so had to look. He'd never been this close to young men before—wasn't crazy, you know—so he didn't know what to think.

They were different, that's for sure. Their skin colors, like that of the old man, were strikingly different to the pallid gleam of undyed cheese of both Father and Father's army. Theirs was a variety of shades that reminded him of snails, of earth, of autumn leaves—and Jet himself, and many others of Father's godchildren.

"See how clean they are," said Jet. "And clean-shaven. Those Gucci sweatshirts, and those complicated athletic shoes. They're just alienated young men, probably most without jobs since this island has over fifty percent youth unemployment."

Nat couldn't argue. He was great at worrying, but that was his only talent.

The young men were all talking at the same time, gesticulating, laughing in quick staccatos while eating ice cream.

"Yuuhup," boomed Jet, aging Nat half an aeon. But weirdly, none of the men looked toward the table by the door.

"They can't see us?"

"Who knows? Maybe if they wanted to. They look past us. Remember, we're not only tourists, but *old*."

"I don't look old," spat Nat. "Tell you what looks old. A human baby. Now that wrinkled thing. Not any of us can match it."

"True, but they know it's not old. And they're programmed to love it no matter how hideous and chilling it looks, whereas we..." Jet shook sadly.

At that, Nat felt enough of a twinge of affection for his brother to do something he had never thought he would. But now he trusted him enough to take the chance. He turned away and then turned back. "Do they work? Do they make me lovable?"

"To the folks back home you mean?" Jet motioned a regretful *no way*. "Don't forget, Nat. They're a lost cause. That's why we're here." He reached over and gently took the two large blue eyes out of Jet, trying to control his horror.

I wonder if I did pick wrong.

The grizzled old man was looking Jet's way, grinning wildly and holding up a soup tureen filled with four new flavors, but Jet was now too worried to notice.

He'd picked the venue—the other side of the earthly world from home, on an island that promised pure paradise—from the brooding, smoking caldera, to the shadowed knife-edged valleys and peaks, to the forests being slowly smothered by a vine that mankind planted and whose vegetable-like fruits they hunt to bake, smothered by cheese sauce—but the vine only spreads like a god born with Manifest Destiny in its mouth. How quaint and amusing!

He'd planned for everyone to meet here first, in this amazingly unhorrific ice cream place smack in the middle of Saint-Denis, the island's big smoke—just a small town with pretty much nothing to do but eat ice cream, he had read. There were of course, tourists, who will go to the ends of the earth for ice cream. But this hole-in-the-wall parlor was strictly local, and not only that, but frequented by "gangs of young disaffected youths" he had read in a one-star review—perfect, he had thought. He'd assumed that none of them would know who his family was, let alone his famous father. And in this place, to not know would be to not fear.

Plus—and he hadn't thought of it before—he and Nat were undeniably *old* and therefore, invisible to the young. That sorta hurt, but—

Suddenly, the air was split by "Some... waaare over the rain... bow"

Nat grabbed his phone. "Yes... no... yes, yes."

His protoplasm shook. "That was Firstborn himself. He's ready to blow because every street's a one-way going the wrong way and he's in a rental car with the side-view mirrors bashed off, and you can only see the street signs by looking backwards, and—"

"Did you tell him how to get here?"

"How should I know?"

"So whadya say yes to?"

"That he doesn't know where he is."

Jet held back a sigh. If Nat were a Swiss Army knife, he wouldn't have a blade.

Although they'd never, of course, met, Jet assumed by Firstborn's rental of one of the toilet-bowl-size Citroens offered on the island, that this sibling could indeed shapechange at will. Jet hadn't known that this first godchild of their father had the ability to really blow. But as Jet and Nat made their way along the clogged and twisted streets, Jet saw a column of steam rising, and rushed towards it. A crowd had surrounded a small, unloved car with its lid as wide open as a Xhugar's maw. The car was spewing like something vigorously disagreeing with being digested.

"Ssss," hissed Nat, pointing to the park across the street. "That must be them."

He was right. A 'man' with an unmistakable glower was standing by a palm tree, and beside him a host of siblings. Jet couldn't help thinking of how they all must have shrink-fitted into that car.

He walked up to Firstborn and extended greetingly. "Glad you got here," he added. "I'm Jet. This here is Nat."

"Hilarion T. Moody," said Firstborn. At that, the rest introduced themselves.

"The Acme."

"O."

"Durian Durian."

"Heart Emoji."

"Shawn."

"Epiphany."

"Pun."

"Vajyna."

etc.

There were twenty-two in all, and no one mentioned that almost all had changed their identities from those awkward and frankly ugly names bestowed upon them by their father as additional curses of birth. By the time the twelfth and thirteenth had said respectively, "Gigantic" and "Gluten-Free," Jet figured that their former multi-syllabic nonsense names had given them no training, and now they were all just grasping at popularity. The only siblings who hadn't changed their names looked embarrassed and caught out, as if it had never occurred to them . . . but they were such lesser gods, it was surprising they pitched up. Jet hadn't thought to invite them, and only faintly remembered them from a footnote in one of those thick-and-convoluted-as-brains paeans of praise to Father.

For a while everyone stood around awkwardly. Then they began to 'mix'. From the polite little jabs and self-effacing brags most uttered, Jet was disappointed to surmise that the motivation for them coming to this unprecedented sibling retreat was a low-life form of curiosity—that which humans harbor in their decision to go to reunions. Each godchild of the Father here hoped that all the others had done worse, been more hated and reviled in a way that was disrespectful, not loaded with fear. For fear gave power. He himself had never felt powerful, only despised.

All his life he was supposed to be this ancient awful

deity—a god. Instead, he'd felt he had less power than old chewing gum. But he'd assumed that some of the rest of them—certainly Firstborn, uh, Moody, would truly be a god, a deity who would save them all from perpetual Ignominium. Yes, they were all spawned in the bile duct connected to the brain of their mentally deranged father. Yes, they were all rejected at birth as being hideous fiends while Father had been held up as a model during his life, and turned before he was properly mouldering in his grave, into a revered god complete with the whole panoply: worshippers, devotees, life-stylers, High Priest, tributes heaped upon tributes; and even festivals to honour, weirdly, the day he emerged messily from his mother, as mortals tend to. No one questioned the life of the former man, who might have had and been stirred by the most unspeakable halitosis, or jealousies. No one sought to peek behind the altar into his motivations. Who knew the real story about his offspring who he to his profit, tormented and slandered? All of them at this meeting had been incomparably damaged by Father's need to make up logorrheaic lies about them—*thereby to gain sympathy as being tormented by his children? Who knows? Why should anyone care? Why do people back home still care, care enough to hate us, of all creations?*

"Our father, whose art's in heaven," said Pun, breaking Jet's spiral into despair. "I say again, Our father whose art's in heaven, horrorifying is thy fame."

"Howifying," corrected someone small (without name tags, remembering the lessers in this constellation of stars was proving impossible).

"Jet." Moody's voice carried, and it trembled. "Get us somewhere appropriate."

"At your command." Jet didn't know what was eating Moody. They were all being totally ignored by the populace, which was eating ice creams, singing, sitting on benches and kissing, walking a variety of tiny dogs, and in a small pavilion, tangoing in romantic, sensualist pairs with a style that would have given Father a final bilific fit, probably big enough to produce triplets. Oh, why hadn't the tango caught on in Mass!? Ah, the dogs. There were two being friendly to Moody, who was clearly not knowing if their overtures were in friendship or hunger.

Hot, wet, slimy, frozen waste, bubbling, aethereal. Jet chose the huge brooding uninviting caldera in the center of the island, a furnace that was unlit at the moment. Its basin was as ugly, bare, and depressing as their father's soul. But this place was a perfect retreat. No one with little dogs would disturb this retreat. No one would come at all.

They met in the middle of the bare ground, as bare as, Vajyna declared, "Planet Zil." The heat was unforgiving, but Moody liked the tropics, so that was why Jet had picked this island, that and a weakness he realized he should not reveal, for he hadn't known before the antipathy of every sibling except Pun, to word-play. This island had not only a tragic history that appealed to Jet, starting out its written history with slaves torn from their homes and lands and shipped out to here to work on the coffee plantations—but its name is Reunion Island (or, for the unsophisticated natives, *Ile de la Réunion*). Jet had always been partial to resonance. Now he hoped no one learned the island's name. It's not like any of them had ever met before, so it was the wrong name anyway.

"Hey!" Nat prodded him. "This is your party, and they're all getting restless."

Nat was right. An ominous groan was starting to rise from the center of the crowd, where one of the uninviteds was speaking as if this were a conference. "... and so if you would like to join with me as victims of verbal and mental abuse—"

Not only that. This empty cauldron, this old volcano that could blow at any moment, was being invaded by armies of ants, streaming down from the top, crawling along the base towards them from all directions.

"They're coming for us!" screamed Shawn.

"They wouldn't know we exist." Moody's scorn was withering.

"You're so right," said—*omg!* Jet's very thoughts petrified.

"Pleased to meet you," said the man who had managed to sneak up without anyone noticing. "I assume you are the great Cth—"

"The Firstborn, Hilarion T. Moody."

"Of course," said the man, smiling smoothly. "How do I address you?"

"You're not sending me anywhere!"

"He wouldn't dare, HT," said Jet. "This Indiana Jones creature—"

"I beg to differ. This is a genuine Akubra I mail-ordered from an ad in the *New Yorker*."

"Sorry. This mail-orderer—"

The man pushed Jet back as if Jet had been a book on a table that the guy had ceased referencing, for the moment.

"I'm surprised you don't know me," he said, striking an academic-author pose. "Now?"

He registered no response.

"Well, you should thank your stars I tracked you here. Just what am I saying that you can understand? Do you know the word 'understand'? How many fingers am I holding out?"

"We can cognisize the pants offa you, mister. What is it you want?" Jet looked to Nat, the physically stronger of the two of them. This man might need physical attention. But Nat was so obviously confused that he had either put himself into a self-induced trance of escapism or more likely, slipped back into his natural state of vacuity.

"I don't *want* anything," said the man "any more than knowledge. You would know, if you had read *anything* in the past ten years, that I'm the world's foremost deologist. and a trailbreaker in the new field of deography. I'm Doctor—"

"You're not from around here," said Moody, who had started to glower. "And you speak too much like Father's followers for my comfort."

"He's a spy!" screamed one of the uninvited.

"I am a scientist," he said. "You should consider it an honor to be studied by me. Now if you would prefer not to be interviewed at the present time, I'll just put these tracking—"

"He speaks Massachusetts!" screeched the same uninvited—her, his, shis, or its last emission.

"We wish to be alone," said Moody.

"To confer. Absolutely."

"Alone from *you*," Jet cut in. He led the self-described Doctor away under Firstborn's watchful eyes.

"Look," Jet said. "Maybe one day you could do us a service, but today we're all meeting each other for the first time. If you know anything about our life histories, you know they're all horrific. You *do* know we're supposed to be malevolent?"

"That's one reason you interest me."

"Wow. You should study *you*. Why aren't you petrified in your terror?"

The man wrinkled his nose. "Fear is not an option for a scientist."

"But..." Jet felt so embarrassed, he almost couldn't ask, but he had to know. "How can you stand our stenches?"

"Stenches?"

"Our foul primordial stinks?"

"You don't stink, but hang on. I can tell you..." He patted his pants-of-many-pockets, and fished out a suspicious-looking instrument. "With this gas chro—"

"You're not gonna gas me!"

"No no no. Look. I'll put it on me. See? Safe as water." The scientist shoved the instrument back in his pocket and velcroed it in. "Don't worry," he said to Jet, smiling. "We'll cross that bridge later. "And you smell like violets."

"Violence." That confirmed Jet's fears. "It must be hideous, unspeakable, cacodaemoniacally ghastly, stink—"

"Violets. A lovely spray of flowers."

Jet's insides fluttered. He wanted to envelope the man, he

was so touched.

"Leave it with me," he said. "I'll get in touch with you to analyze our DNA, our patrichondria, whatever, if you share your findings only with us. But hey, how do you speak so well, and yet you don't hate us?"

"I'm from Tasmania."

"Where's that?"

"Near Transylvania."

"Philadelphia, Transylvania?" That sounded suspiciously close to home.

"No, Transylvania Islands. Used to be called the Malingerers."

Jet felt reassured enough to wish the nosy scientist well. Perhaps one day... but he could be helpful now. Jet had seen that the armies of ants were not ants at all, but people— hikers, to be exact. Long lines of them, hard and muscled as old apple trees. None of the hikers noticed the group, but the group had noticed them.

"D'you have a place on this island that is the retreat we want?"

"This island's just a pimple on the ocean. Craggy and wild, to be sure. But so small, the whole place is inhabited. This isn't full-on tourist season, but it's infested with them. And then there's the local people. But that's just the start. There's enough deities on this island to last me a lifetime; and spirits; and intransigent ancestors; and a whole passel of obnoxiously self-righteous saints, if I do say so myself."

"There must be *someplace*," Jet wheedled, cringing at how that sounded, but he was desperate. "Just for a one-nighter."

"Well... the night, you say?" The scientist took his hat off and turned it round in his hands. "If you go up the mountainside from any of the villages, you won't hit people at all, and once above the trails, even the shrines stop. "But do be careful of the shoo shoo, and never sleep."

"Thanks," said Jet, lightly pushing him away. While the rest of the group were merely disorientatedly restless, Jet felt the hot glare of Firstborn (Jet couldn't think of him on a first-name basis, and both 'HT' and 'Moody' were hard to get used to—Jet *had* been kinda afraid to meet him—that almost believable terror-striking reputation.)

The island was so filled with craggy peaks and little villages precariously perching halfway up the sharply shadowed valleys, that it was dead easy for Jet to lead them to the promised one-night-land, only relative moments away.

A steep slope shined emerald green from that vine Jet had read about, the one that was biblically fruitful, the one with fruits that hung from the tendrils. And the fruits looked strangely familiar. They looked like Shawn! Shawn himself—that slightly greasy semi-hard green skin sparsely but definitely bristling all over with two-day growth, all over its fissured globose head-shaped body. The fruits, some twice the size of a man's head, hung pendulous at packed intervals on the twisted vine when young. When ready, they had clearly fallen to the earth, only to plant themselves there, rather like an army's dead plants its bodies for others to be fruitful on. In this case, the green Shawnlike things sprouted new vine, which rose to cover yet more of the slope. The slope had strange cants to it—like tents poking up out of it. They were tall trees that the vine had climbed up and tented over.

It all would have made Jet's skin crawl if his physiology had taken that route. He did shudder. For the first time in his life, he felt irrational fear. Of what? Only what he'd never seen before.

He watched an old man with a machete that flashed in the sunlight, trudge up the track below, and venture slightly into the emerald slope. There were a few sounds of whacking, and the man emerged with an armful of Shawn-things.

"Those must be the things they cover with cheese sauce," Jet said. No one was listening, but that didn't matter. He'd reassured himself.

They were all so exhausted that when the shadows fell,

even the chatteriest of the group went quiet. Jet listened to some snore, and was surprised that they could. But he didn't have time to be surprised for long.

Just before total darkness fell, his ols picked up a scent brought up from the track below—the rotting fruits of a wild little self-planted tree, the fruits of which he knew must be red as Moody's fifth eye, the fruits of which must have been crushed into that ice cream that was what living should be about, that had stirred Jet so much, he had actually tasted for the very first time, and had grown ols to smell . . . omg! those fruits were near.

I'm never going home...

The chou chou (pronounced *shoo shoo*) had also been torn from His, Her, Sher, or Its home across the seas and brought to Reunion along with more cheap labour. Being such a grower, it, powerlessly for a while, fed exclusively, like cattle food, the poor imported workers from South America, Indo-Asia, Africa, who cut cane in the fields, tended the finickety vanilla, boiled in molasses plants and rum distilleries, served the rich for a pittance, but knew how to eat—whose decendents now have a reputation for being kiss-your-fingers world-fusion cuisinartisans.

That anything tastes good smothered with cheese sauce is such a known fact, it isn't worth mentioning. But it is true that chou chou smothered in cheese sauce, and baked till your saliva runs, if you're human, is a common and much-loved dish in Reunion. And with chou chous for the taking, even the poor can and do eat well.

That old machete-wielding man regularly climbed the very slope described earlier, where he hunted chou chous to sell in the village. He did so the very next morning after the campout of Jet et al. His eyes were bleached and weak, but even if they'd been eaglish, he would have seen no one, and not because he wasn't from Massachusetts. The chou chou isn't known in New England as a deity, but it sure has power.

By morning, every one of Jet's siblings in that retreat was only sustenance for a vine, its tendrils having reached, found, sucked and budded with a prolifickness it had never enjoyed before.

A month or so later, the old man took a particularly tooth-some-looking chou-chou bake out of the oven. Its top gleamed red and gold, beaded with grease, and it smelled divine.

He lived alone. He set his table for one. And he ate the whole chou chou bake all by himself.

He could be forgiven, being old as he was, for not noting that the whole time he was cutting and chewing, cutting and chewing, the diminishing surface of the bake was bubbling, but the cheese sauce was so silky smooth that the cheese-sauce-coated fingers frantically twiddling out from the bake made not a sound. And though the old man had no teeth, he had no problems with devourance. Nat et al. had not a verte-brate amongst them, though some would have been rubbery, if the old man hadn't been such a natural cook.

And that could have been the end of that—the god Chou Chou in all His Vineness, encompassing more deities and increasing his number and who knows what, if there weren't a couple more turnips in that pot.

Probably 50 years ago, a man in this little cottage ate something that disagreed with his mortality—a chou chou bake that he'd made himself. He was a great cook, and the bake tasted quite divine. Since that day he hasn't aged a day. Immortality is a fine thing when you are young and hand-some, but he was already old—this old man.

Now he knows he's not only immortal, but a god with growing strength. What can he do with it? He never knew before.

But now that he's got all the godchildren but one in him, he has terrible indigestion.

The night is long and full of rumbles.

Jet hadn't been able to properly lie down, not with the scent rising in the night... till... It commanded him. It pulled him down to it, down the treacherous chou-chou-vinous slope as if the chou chou were a mere vegetable victim fit for slugs, and it—that ol-maddening sinuously writhing body of smell—were a mythic siren—and he, Jet, famous as an unspeakably terrifying deity—he, Jet: a mere man.

He had to creep, ooze, flit his way down the slope and along the path his ols told him to take. Within an hour of his siblings all passing into unconsciousness and simultaneously into the pitiless coursing visceral streams of the Chou Chou, he had found the source of the scent—first, the rotting fruits lying on the path like so many precious Firstborn's eyes. He fell upon them greedily, and almost grenaded in his joy.

They also, had a curious effect, making him their servant. For they wasn't *they*, but the goddess herself, Psidium c. Sabine. The She herself. Throughout history she has crept into human legend, through every silent 'p' and 'c'; through the irresistible, rubylipped Guinevere; in the luscious body of the fruit known on Reunion simply as *Goyavier* (and by those quick to compound a name without knowledge, as *Strawberry Guava*, though a strawberry is an anaemic lump compared to her—and *Goyavier de Chine*, though she no more came from China than Jet does from Brazil). But what does she care of inaccuracies, She, this 'fresh, slightly rank and earthy' (according to Jet's ols, which became amazingly sophisticated in no time), red red lascivious *Goyavier* to whom Reunion's islanders throw a worshipful festival every year: the *Fête des Goyaviers*.

To be worshipped! Jet for all his godness, had only experienced the opposite, not that he was filled with envy. Quite the opposite. He loves to say her name to feel her roll on his parts.

Gwha yah-vee Yay!

Jet works at Her command—and in return, she deigns

to let him taste her, exercise his ols upon her, lick her frigid body till he's never sated but always wanting more . . . But he is as happy as any madman ruled by Love.

Monsieur O____, the old man in the ice cream parlour, was delighted to go into partnership with 'Zhet', who proved himself quickly. Indeed, the old man saw in the younger, not only someone whose taste was divine, but who ran the hangout as if he were born to. Sometimes the passionate perfectionist, who had thought no one could ever thrill to his calling as much as he always had, stood back and watched Zhet decorating the goyavier glacés with flowers, fruits, candles, fresh and fragrantly rotting goyaviers—and a tear would run down the grizzled cheek, for the old man knew his prayers to his own private god had been answered in the most surprising way. This 'Zhet' didn't fool him one little bit. He knew to the roots of his last four teeth, that this 'man' wasn't a man at all, but his guardian angel.

As to the little place itself, even though it still has no sign other than a board saying *Glacés*, and the street is too narrow for most tourists, they would liposuction themselves thin to get in if the place weren't already even more packed than ever with all those nice young men who've got nowhere else welcoming to go. And now that Zhet is running things, Monsieur O, wrinkle-faced, as toothy as a suckulous infant, but otherwise forever a young romantic—can take time off to:—tango.

As to that forever-old and seedy-looking chou-chou hunter and baker, who encompassed Nat et al. in one super-size meal—he now resides in a small town in Massachusetts. He is more unhappy than ever, but he was driven to go by a force he cannot explain. Of course he hasn't a hope of finding work. He lives on the street, his cottage a cardboard box, and *his recycled real-estate sign asks: Pleese spare $3.98 fore un boddel ouv cheeze sausse.*

He would just be one of the great unnoticed—quietly starving, unable to wash—but for a certain scientist who has followed him here, and keeps tags on him.

THE SLIME:
A LOVE STORY

AT a time of life when the slime was mature but not brittle, it fell in love—a dangerous sentiment and an alien one, but when has love cared? From being a blob of sturdy equanimity throughout, love changed the slime so that it softened to runny on the inside, crusty on the out.

Alarmed, the slime begged for advice, but all the dust in the room, lintballs on the furniture, scrap paper, crumbs, rubber bands, and even the oddbent paperclips, were useless or *worse*.

Shocked, the slime fled.

After almost falling victim three times, it found in a place undisturbed for many years, a book with a brittle fossil of glue clinging to the spine. At the slime's touch, the pages fell to

THE ART OF CORRESPONDENCE: LOVE LETTERS

The slime followed all of the chapter's advice. It copied all the sample letters from one side of the affair, only changing names and omitting certain phrases, like "dear girl".

My dear Miss Searles, the slime wrote. I can no longer restrain myself from writing to you, dearest and best. I love you so much that I cannot find words. My heart has long been yours, as I will own. Just send one kind word to Your sincere adorer.

The slime signed the letters *Cedric W. McCrae* and addressed the envelopes to *Miss Viola Searles*. A love letter, the slime had learnt, must have proper names for the 'to' and 'from'. Cedric cheered it, and Viola suited its love.

When the whole pile's-worth in the chapter had been written, answering every permutation of reply, expressing every occasion for sentiment including a death in the family, the time came to post them. But though the slime had carefully copied the addresses in the book, the preposterousness of the project suddenly glared, brighter than clean paper.

The object of the slime's love, the slime suddenly remembered, not only *could not read*, but most probably had *no dear friends, nor useful advisors*. The object of the slime's love would never know it cared.

The slime fled yet again, looking for answers to its state of love. It found sympathy from a piece of amber on a deserted beach, but no answers. It shadowed a shoe, actually the something stuck to the bottom of it, but the slime missed the moment when the shoe scraped the something off. The slime then wasted a lot of time shadowing the shoe for nothing.

The slime was possessed by love. It never stopped thinking of love, though one day when the slime cried "Viola!", as it was wont to do, and someone asked, "Viola who?", as ones often did, the slime could not remember who, nor even what. All the slime could remember was love, not the object of its love.

But love wrought yet more changes, this dangerous love did. The slime's outside crust now extended so far to the inside that the runny part was just a tiny dot. Then the crusty part began to crack, and that hurt more than love.

Love caused this change, the slime ah-ha'd, and began to hate its love.

The slime warmed to hate, and soon hated with a heat so hot that the crusty part melted from the inside out till one day the slime was equanimity again, with nary a crusty bit. The slime moved this way and that, felt smooth throughout, and resiliated in joy.

Hate, you did this, the slime cried out. *Hate, you blessedly restored me.* After that, the slime traveled the land extolling the virtues of hate.

"Hate for what?" others asked. The slime looked too youthful to be wise, too healthy to be stupid.

"For love!" the slime always answered, which sounded so wise that no-one dared question that.

The slime felt so smooth and firm and confident and full of thanks for its lesson learnt that it traveled now only the high road, to adventure and extol. You might have seen it then. You might have heard it.

The slime completely forgot its love. Its fame grew. One day when it was delivering one of its six set speeches—this one had made crowds roar oh, hundreds of times… brrrrrr! *Talking hate is dangerous.* Cool words. (Needed?) The slime suddenly felt itself all over—cold and brittle as a marble slab. It stopped its speech and went on its way again. The slime renounced the word. Deed only, became its life. Hate constant, pure and true. And by hating with such a heat, the slime became its own true self again, youthfully soft, and even softer. You might have seen it then, this silent traveler on the high road.

And so one shimmering midday when the road felt only one traveler, the slime, hating constant, pure and truer than ever, melted altogether, not to be seen nor heard again.

That brittle winter, the road felt something tight. Something pulling on its body in a certain place. It looked there and saw nothing, but the thing still pulled. So the road bent its body just so, and back again. And sure enough, the pulling thing flaked off.

The pulling thing was the frozen slime, now broken into bits.

Oddly, or maybe it was fate, next to the pieces was the thing that had been scraped off the shoe so long ago.

A gust of wind, or possibly something else, moved the

thing that had been scraped off the shoe, and then moved it some more, so that the thing moved like a broom round the bits of slime till they were all one pile. A pile of frozen slime bits.

And then the thing that had been scraped off the shoe fell upon the pile of frozen slime bits. And though winter was brittle, the thing was resilience itself.

Come spring, it melted the slime again. It melted the slime so much, they made a whole together.

That was a long time ago. But unless I've heard wrong, they are still together.

CARE AND SENSIBILITY

T WAS a long flight, so the loop of that phone call must have played a thousand times in Justine's head. As it was, she hoped she wasn't too late.

It started alarmingly. "Tell her I'm busy," she'd heard her mother say. "Oh, lemme have it. Get the damn thing over with."

"Yeah, I'm alive," yelled Simone Orbeville Coulomb, Justine Coulomb's mom, into the phone.

Justine's hand shook, she was so worried. She'd never been to this place her mom had picked, but in the last three monthly calls, the woman had been manageable. Justine asked gently, "Have you taken—"

"A lover? Not that I've noticed." That sarcasm—healthy as ever. "She doesn't tell me I'm forgetful. She doesn't ask me if I've taken my pills. She just gives them to me. And she not only loves opera, but begs me to sing."

She? "Mom—"

"Don't Mom me. You're rolling your eyes, aren't you? She never rolls her eyes even when, well, never."

Justine's skin prickled.

"And," cooed her mother, "I finally have my Scrabble opponent. She's so good, I don't care if she wins. She doesn't know how to gloat. Or," she added ominously, "sigh."

That did it. This was what Justine had feared for years. Some wily interloper pretending to care a way into the venerable and infinitely trying Simone Orbeville Coulomb's considerable Will.

That voice of hers tore its way through the lines: "You got something to say?"

"Just seeing how you're doin'," Justine chirped.

"Don't bother. Justine here makes sure I'm fine."

"Justine?"

"Quite a coincidence." Simone Orbeville Coulomb dropped the phone on what must have been the floor. It was picked up and the conversation extinguished but not before her only child heard that nasty chuckle turn into a wracking cough.

No matter how many times the conversation played in Justine's head, she came to the same conclusion: Mom, you left me no choice.

Justine arrived, dehydrated, smelly and wrinkled, straight out of a taxi—at 4:12 pm Sunday afternoon, what she'd heard was the quietest time of the week at a place like this.

Indeed, there was only a pleasant-faced but rather somnolent woman at Reception, who upon hearing that this visitor was some friend of that Coloumb woman, said, "She on fourth floor," before dropping her head to daydream.

There was no one else in sight, which was fine by Justine. She took the first corridor left and walked till she found the janitorial room, where she picked out a fine mop.

Then she explored a bit, poking her head into a room where a few uniformed workers were listening to some foreign music and variously knitting, playing cards, and reading. No "Justine" here, she concluded. Too poor for opera. Too foreign for Scrabble.

Exploring further, she could see little signs of why her mother had chosen this place. There were lots of classy little details—a discarded empty outside one inmate's door: a '67 Chateau d'Yquem. A coffee table bearing piles of *Vogue*, *Scientific American*, *Fortune*. Thick carpet and good upholstery, as if this weren't a warehouse for incontinents. No sound of dueling televisions.

In fact, the corridor was empty and all was so quiet that when she came upon the door that said "Staff Charging Room," she almost didn't open it, but curiosity made her want to look in to what must be some in-house court room for wayward workers.

She opened the door, and almost dropped the mop. You read about this stuff but it's always in other places. There were five of them in here, a light on each "forehead" blinking red. Even in their passive state, their bodies were strangely attractive. Their eyes were huge, adorable. Diabolically trustworthy.

Their nametags were just like the human workers. Merilee, Francis, Odette, Samuel, Xavier.

She half-suppressed a retch, slammed the door, found the elevator and punched the button of the lift for the fourth floor.

She came out swinging. The mop's head was as large as Medusa's.

Just as she expected, her mother was in bed.

Justine had flown here sure that her mother hadn't changed the Will yet. It would only take at most, two blows to provide closure.

But what must have been "Justine"—it stood beside the bed, a Scrabble piece in its "hand."

Justine lunged at it. With the first hit of the mop's handle, she heard a satisfying crunch. Pulling it away, the mop's locks caught in a "shoulder" joint, ripping it open.

Two more swings, and the abomination, this pretender to her Daughterhood, was jerking obscenely on the floor.

Two bony hands gripped her wrist. Her mother had managed to get out of bed. "Please," she wailed. "Stop hurting her." It was the first time Justine ever saw her mother cry.

"How could you?" she said, hurt more than she thought she could be. She turned around and stomped hard on its "chest."

"I forgive you," it said.

"I won't," said Justine's mother, unwisely.

CARDOONS!

"**M**ix some string into a bowl of sick, and pour that on a plate."

"That's enough, Riri," said her father, reaching for another Milkmaid from the box. "Your amma goes to so much trouble to fix you a healthy meal."

Let's trade troubles! thought Roariferex Glak, for the punishment in the Glak lair was: "If you don't eat your cardoons now, you'll get twice as much tomorrow." And she knew from experience that cardoons were double trouble multiplied by infinity. Roariferex, by the way, is the name she was given when she hatched. She had to put up with what her parents called her, but she was *Roar* to her friends.

Roar's chin trembled with indignation. *Why!* she thundered silently, *do I get into trouble for what my body does?* Her throat would jam shut and her stomach jump. Then her teeth—all one hundred and fifty of them—would close so tight that they met in a jagged clamp, her top front fangs pressed down so hard over her chin scales that each scale's root was rimmed with blood.

She could close her eyes and it *still* happened, just at the thought of putting any part of that dead flop and slither on her tongue. It happened even if she dipped her smallest talon into that humungous mountain just for her, of: gloop-grey, smelliverous, and slimily *yeggigh* as the last frog in a carton forgotten in the fridge—a heaped peak of it—forbidding and compulsory, and unfair as parents who don't eat it themselves—*cardoons!*

She stopped breathing, stuck in her fork, twirled and pulled up the first dripping writhing monstermassful to get it over with fast, pushed it in past her teeth, swallowed—and was caught.

A clump of stems stayed up in her mouth while the bottom tugged from somewhere in her depths, like having your legs yanked while your wings are stuck above two rocks. Tears sprang out of her eyes as her throat clutched the rope. Grey slime dripped from her chin.

Her father leapt from his chair as well as he could, and lumbered over. He swung his arm out, and with all his puny strength, whacked Roar's back. Halfway down the long drop of her throat, its muscles snapped the rope, yanking down half the clump in a gulp that hurt. The other half shot out of her mouth.

Roar wiped her eyes. In front of her, the mountain loomed. She would have blubbered snot if she had noticed the new topping she would have to eat again, extra-glistening and bubbly from her own choke.

"Would you like some water, Wiwi?" asked her mother. "It helps slip gulps," she said carefully, from experience.

Roar nodded. It took her seventy gruesome gulpfuls. Mrs. Glak watched every one, her brows knitted in a sympathetic grimace.

At the last gulp, Mrs. Glak declared: "You can't expect something that is healthy to taste good."

And she reached into the box, pulled out a Milkmaid, and stuffed it in her mouth. Its smell was droolicious. Even the picture of milkmaids on the box-top almost made Roar wish she were old enough already to eat them. But the picture on the side made her turn away before it fed her nightmares.

"Parents!" she mumbled. "If they were *my* children…"

Roar's father was relaxing on the sofa, one hand wrapped

around a cold can of Bloodbrew. On the big screen, dragons of the Old Days made the God of Thunder quake. Great wings filled the picture. The sound of those wings flapping was loud enough to drown out Now.

"Those were the days," her father was fond of saying, just before, "It's a mite chilly," or "Fancy a bite, dear?"

Over in her chair, Roar's mother was engaged in her favourite activity, knitting. Her second most favourite was spinning. Her spinning wheel and boxes of the stuff she spun into yarn were piled around her chair. The lair was filled with her knitted presents—blankets piled up that no one used because the lair had push-button heating. Tea cosies warmed empty teapots—the Glaks drank no tea. Roar's mother knitted sweaters and socks and blankets and gloves that she sent away to needy dragons in foreign lands. But most of all, she loved knitting for Mr. Glak, who was never seen out of her hand-spun, hand-knitted original creations. He even wore them to bed.

Roar looked at her father stretched out on the sofa, the can of Bloodbrew rising and falling on his stomach, and felt a bit less resentful about the cardoons. *Maybe it is true*, she thought, *that if you eat cardoons from an early age* (as Roar had since a baby) *your wings will grow and develop* ("in twelve different ways") *and your claws and talons will grow.*

And, thought Roar, *I might, one day, maybe, just for a couple of flaps, fly.* Well, that last wish was as silly as her becoming a real Dragonair—a Capable of Terror, Rampage and Fire—most Wondrous Dragon of Old.

"Amma," called her father. "You peckish?"

"I'm working, dear," said Roar's mother. "But I'll get you a bite." She waddled to the kitchen and came back with a box of Salties and another can beaded with cold sweat, that she placed at Mr. Glak's elbow. He patted her behind affectionately. Roar watched and felt a mixture of happiness for them, and revulsion. *How can they love each other when they look like that?*

Her father's scales didn't properly cover his skin any more. His arms and legs were thin and as muscle-free as if he'd worked to achieve it. And on his feet were... shoes. Roar's mother had developed "knitter's finger" and was actually thankful, saying it "helps me cast the yarn", whatever that meant. She also wore shoes to hide her feet, and for this Roar was thankful. But all this was nothing compared to the rest. They both had a *behind*—thick and wide like a cushion—under the tail. And their tails! Bent at the base, Mr. Glak's to the left, and Mrs. Glak's to the right.

Roar had never got used to knowing that the only mystery about growing up was which way her tail would bend. That she would grow to have a behind instead of a sloped sleek shape, that her tail would grow to be, not the slashing weapon of a dragon of Old but like that handle at the sink that her mother liked to use her elbows on. *You can't beat reality.* Her claws and talons would get thinner and weaker, till they just broke off at the ends of her fingers and toes. And as for wings...

The biggest reason Roar hated eating her cardoons is that she didn't believe they would work. It's not like anyone pretended cardoons were magic, but really! Might as well snort three times and make a wish. No, cardoons wouldn't save her from growing up and looking like a mockery of any dragon of Old. Not that her fate to grow up, therefore to look repulsive, gave her nightmares. For after all, she'd decided: *Looking bad doesn't kill you, or there'd be no adults alive, let alone loving each other.*

Roar was frightened for her parents. Why didn't they *look* at those boxes they were always digging into? The top of the Milkmaids showed the same plump sweet milkmaid on every box, and the top of the Salties showed the same salty sailor comically brandishing his useless cutlass. But the ads for Milkmaids and Salties could have bragged: *Collect us!* promising truthfully about the sides: *No two terrifying close-up pictures alike. A different set of WARNINGs on every box.*

The box her parents had just finished to the last little foot said:

Eating Milkmaids is a danger to your health.
Your mouth will develop lips.
Your bones will become droolicious goo.
You will grow hair, and it will be long and yellow.
Your eggs will be rotten when laid, if you are lucky.
Every Milkmaid you eat will bring you one step closer
to a soft and smooth complexion.

And if that wasn't enough to scare you off, every box of Milkmaids said, in big black letters:

MILKMAIDS KILL

As for the pictures...

Salties were the same. Forbidden till you're grown-up, deliciously tempting at any age—and not only deadly, but terrifying to see just how.

Even the Ingredients List made the scales rise on the top of Roar's head. *Reconstituted?* What does that mean? No WARNING explained, so Roar guessed. *Ingredients with names like maltoambidextrose and numbers like D873 can't be safe.* Most of all, the sweet softness of the Milkmaids and the tongue-tingling tang of the Salties should have warned any dragon off. *Nothing tasting that good can be safe.*

But anyway, Roar wished she lived in the Old Days, when Dragons ate real milkmaids spiced with fear, snatched fresh from their field or dairy. Back then, dragons ruled the air and shook the mountains with their roars. A Dragon of Old didn't eat anything with labels, didn't live in heated lairs, didn't shop, didn't settle down together. Back then, they had no name or only one name, no Mr. and Mrs. in the Old Days. No dragon needed to see some ingredients list on a Dragon-slayer charm to be aware of it and not only WARNED but ready to fight against it with tooth and claw and fire.

For back then, that charm was foul indeed, even in the

hands of that shortcutting dragon hunter Glabarious the Sneak against the first of the lazy easy-living-loving dragons, Slothful. Now the charm was lost, as were dragon hunters. Now people were soft, but so were dragons. Roar was sometimes impatient with her father's love of those flying dragons of Old—those (to be honest) screen stars costumed with sewn-on scales, shaking their heads with scripted fury, gaping their mouths wide to throw their painted-in-later flames.

The contrast between those dragons that Mr. Glak dreamed he was and Mr. Glak himself—between Dragonair (the one he cheered the most) and Mrs. Glak—between even the comics of that make-believe Old and any real dragon today was so great that Roar sometimes got up mid-evening and stomped off to bed so she didn't stand in front of the screen and say, "They make you look worse than you are. You don't even *walk* anywhere. And no dragon has flown since ... when!?"

But Roar was angry at herself, too, for dreaming of flying dragons. She'd wake remembering a slow flapping. Her mother once got someone in to inspect the lair complex ventilation, but they mustn't have fixed it. "Fans just do that sometimes," said the technician.

Roar ended her evening curled against her father on the sofa. Mr. Glak snorted convulsively and his toes curled in his shoes as he swooped and grasped in his sleep. Roar was also dreaming, *yah!* But not of an Old One. Roar dreamed of her hero, the one in the poster on her bedlair wall.

Roar opened her eyes and smiled at C. Roar's friends said he was so "Huhaah!", a word that Roar wished she could kill. *Huhaah* made no distinction between C and so many super-popular things, like Talent Time—all those imitators of successful entertainers who are famous at being fake. And those Real'Lore Longer'Lash talon extensions. And those Prey toys that as soon as you pounce on them, experience screambox failure.

And all that stuff that Amma buys at the craft shop and spins into her yarn—reindeer and octopuses, elephants and walruses, storks, lobsters and crocodiles, porcupines by the handful... *And Amma is so "good" at it, she teaches! And then there's those made-up dragons in fake histo-sagas that Affa lives on as if the producers move the pace of his heart by their shows.*

But C is as real as me. And not only that. *No one can do what C does, so he means something to so many, yet how many admit it?* Roar had noticed that when her mother came into her bedlair to inspect for cleanliness, she stayed longer than she had a reason to. So one day Roar secretly watched her gaze at the tattered poster. Mrs. Glak suddenly stood up straighter, slid her jaws around, and went *huff* once. She must have embarrassed herself even though she thought she was alone, because she followed the pathetic empty breath with a fit of coughing,

Roar's father barely approved of the poster, of what he called its "bad influence". Of course Roar had never seen C up closer than in a magazine she found once, shoved under her mother's chair.

With all Roar's heart, she wanted to believe that C really did look like his pictures. Scales shining like a hoard of jewels, green and blue and black and silver, with streaks of gold. No scale lay down flat. They stuck out proudly, defiantly, their points as hard as sword tips, their sides sharp enough to slash. His arms and legs were thick with muscles, his wings so big that they looked unreal, as did his claws and talons that were either fake, as some said, or so real they were worth Roar's dreams. C's great nose flared as though he smelled things not of this tamed world. His eyes were like that time of night when the sun is just fleeing. They glittered like jewels of Old—purple topaz streaked with black. C made Roar shiver, he looked so forbidding. His mane was a ridge of jagged mountains from the top of his head to the tip of his tail, which ended in a spiked club that, in a battle of Old, would have caused Death in a single *flick*. Even Dragonair didn't have scales as glorious, and Dragonair was a make-believed Old.

Sometimes at night, Roar looked from bed at the wall where she knew the poster was, and she begged the picture to be true. Roar had never seen C perform live, of course, and her father had forbidden her to see him on the screen, saying to Roar's mother, "It's unhealthy, Flagra. Better for Riri to know her limits."

Why C was called C was something there was much debate about, as everything in C's life caused gossip and news. But that was his name. C. It was the only thing written on the precious poster, in a new and sharper version of scaly Old Time letters.

"Aren't you going to get out of bed?" said a crusty voice.

"No, Gunkl Fleer," laughed Roar, jumping up and running to wrap her arms around her father's father's grand-father's brother. Though *gunkl* is abbreviated dragon-tongue for *Gregigk Undgkl* (great uncle), no other dragon anyone knew was older than a plain Great Uncle. The Glaks called Fleer "Gunkl" because even *Gregigk Undgkl* is difficult for a dragon who still possesses all one hundred and fifty teeth (and the dragon-tongue for great great uncle is impossible for anyone to say)—and Roar's parents, like most grownups, had false teeth that clicked horribly and then got stuck, fangs locked into fangs, when they said anything with more than one 'g' in it.

"Looking at His Magnificence again, I see," said Gunkl Fleer.

Roar looked up at the ancient dragon's filmy eyes. "How do you know?" she asked. "And I bet he wouldn't like being called His Magnificence."

"I can smell your interest. And it's not what someone's named that makes them."

Roar winced. She certainly knew that. After all, her father's name was Terrorfik Glak, and her mother, Flagration. Everyone except Gunkl Fleer and C had a name that made this life an unfunny joke. Roar hung her head.

"You don't have to make me feel bad, Gunkl. I know my place in history."

"You know nothing. Come," said Fleer. "Let's go to my cave."

Roar found it hard to slow her footsteps enough to keep alongside Gunkl Fleer, who proceeded jerkily—swaying side to side on his bowed legs, his knotted feet and toe talons catching in the decorative flooring, all the way out of the nice lair complex... and around the back side of the mountain... to a crack in the rockface. It opened up to become a cave, so high and dark at the top that it might as well have been roofed by midnight. Somewhere close, water *dripped... dripped... dropped.* This was where Fleer lived now, but from his scars and the stories he had told Roar, he must have stopped in many places, long "Before," as he put it, "any dragon thought that life could be improved by progress and the things of civilized living."

"Don't dawdle out there," he snapped, walking into the gloom. "Chairs and sitting, air con and knitting. Nights gaping at stars on a screen..." Fleer was muttering as he tended to when they came back from Roar's home. There wasn't anyplace to sit. Fleer settled on his haunches on the dank stone. He certainly wasn't padded under his long powerful tail, which flicked once, sending up a spray of cold water. "Lairs soften you!" he huffed. The breath from his disgust left a smoke cloud hovering.

Roar's mouth fell open in awe at that smoke. She never got used to it. No one, but no one, except Fleer, could actually do this anymore. She had sworn solemnly not to tell anyone. In fact, she kept every one of her gunkl's secrets, for they were dangerous and, well... *secrets!*

"What are you looking at?" Fleer demanded. "Remember, you can touch anything and pick anything up."

"Thank you, Gunkl." She walked the length of a saggy and threadbare cloth pinned up here and there. The embroidered picture had once been bright with exotic colours, but it was milky now, filmed over by the works of a thriving community of spiders. Roar tore a hole big enough to look at the face and part of the body in the picture, and was as surprised as she always was at the sight. If Gunkl Fleer had not insisted, Roar wouldn't have believed this could *be* a dragon, let alone...

"Your great love," said Roar, who felt shy to say her name out loud, since she was Gunkl Fleer's secret. "What was she like?"

"Ahh," smiled Fleer. "She could whip the sea into froth, and tie a wave into knots. When she shook her head, she made a sound like a thousand bells. She had shining red and pink scales, and great round eyes, and a wide flat mouth and nose that you might think is ugly—"

"No, I don't!"

"Don't interrupt. I know you must, unless you really are so different from..."

Roar put her hand on Fleer's hard knee, and the dragon who had outlived centuries laid a leathery wing on top of Roar's arm. Roar looked at the talons on that wing, and then at the scars of battles that had left ridges on the thick scales on Gunkl Fleer's limbs. Then Roar looked down and compared feet. Fleer was the only grown-up with bare feet, something he refused to act ashamed about. Fleer's talons on his feet, and the claws on his wings, were scratched dull and aged yellow, and had grown into grotesque shapes like beings with their own minds.

Roar looked at her own neatly curved glossy black talons and claws, and thought of her future. They wouldn't go yellow, but she'd trade. Everything on Fleer's body was hard and dried, curved and scarred, ancienter than anyone—and yet, still dangerous.

"Tell me another story of your old days," Roar asked, and she didn't have to ask twice.

"I wish I could have been you," sighed Roar. "Imagine

swooping down on a village and snatching my own milk-maids, and gobbling them in the air. And do salties really taste better when they're torn from ship's rigging?"

"Yes, they do," chuckled Fleer. "It makes them fluffier."

"And no one told you what was good for you."

"My mother died when I was young," said Fleer. "And my father was away fighting. So nobody cared."

"Oh." For a moment, Roar felt bad, but then she remembered how angry she'd be soon. As soon as the next meal.

"You didn't have to eat cardoons!"

"Is that what's bothering you?"

"That and..." She clamped her mouth shut, wishing she hadn't said anything.

"Huff it out," ordered Fleer.

Roar gulped. "It's the Milkmaids and Salties. That's prac-tically all they eat. I... I don't want them to..."

She squeezed her eyes closed, not able to say more. Already, her stomach felt like there was a fight to the death going on in there. Something tickled her chin. Fleer's leath-ery wing, wiping her tears.

"So you worry," said Fleer, "that the promises on the boxes will happen to them?"

Roar nodded, and then remembered her gunkl's blind-ness. "Yes."

"And you worry that if you hadn't noticed those warn-ings and the promises written there, that nothing bad would happen?"

"How do you know?"

Gunkl Fleer laughed, a big sound that started deep inside and came out warm and misty. It was very infectious, and Roar couldn't help giggling, though she was glad her gunkl didn't see her bright yellow blush.

"The greatest temptation we all face," he said, "is not seeing what we don't want to see. If your mother and father live on Milkmaids and Salties, and don't look at the warn-ings, they won't protect themselves from what's bad. And you telling me doesn't make all those bad things happen just because you're worried that they will."

"But they will, won't they?"

"Too much of anything can hurt you, even if it's comfort. But a bit of this, and a bit of that. Now, that's the way we used to live. And feel my muscles!"

"Or cardoons?"

"What about cardoons?"

"Why don't cardoons have warnings? Why do I have to eat them? I don't see you eating yeggigh, stupid, deadrottlenfrog cardoons."

"So this is where you're leading?" smiled Fleer. "How would you like to go to a concert?"

"Please don't change the subject," said Roar, really disappointed. She had been hoping that her gunkl, even though he was old, would understand. She had hoped that Gunkl Fleer would tell her parents just how wrong they were, and that Roar wouldn't have to live with such unfairness. Gunkl Fleer wouldn't be unfair, Roar was sure of it. So sure that she had almost asked her parents if she could move in with Gunkl Fleer, but every time she planned to, she was safe and warm in bed. She never thought of living here while visiting. There was so much to see here and pick up and explore, but it was all so uncomfortable. Everything was wet and cold, with lots of sharp places that poked into you if you weren't tough like him.

"So you don't want to go to a concert," he shrugged. "You might as well run along. Play some nice imaginary game, safe inside where your mother can watch you."

"I don't want that," she lied. She had wanted just that. Not the mother watching part, but lying on her bed, imagining being someone else. Besides, Gunkl Fleer's ideas of concerts would be as weird as his idea of beauty. Roar looked at the old painting of Fleer's great lost love—that coiled serpent body as thick as a normal dragon's but twice as long. Roar boggled at the total lack of wings, and Roar's eyes narrowed at that swollen flattened face. Roar used to shudder at the sight, but now she tried to see with different eyes—the eyes of someone in love, but more—the eyes of someone who had eaten Vikings for breakfast and Huns for lunch.

"So you don't want to see see," said Fleer.

"See see?"

"Your hero?"

"C! You know about C?"

"I am not blind in the brain, young one."

"But…" stammered Roar, totally confused.

"But nothing," snapped Fleer. "Do you want to go? I'll sit in the back of the crowd, so I won't embarrass you."

"I don't want that!"

Gunkl Fleer was right about the embarrassment. So it doesn't make sense, but a moment after Roar lied again, she really wanted Gunkl Fleer beside her at the concert of the year, almost as much as she wanted to go to the concert so famed and so unique that it had a name: C You at The Mountain.

"See us at the concert," Fleer chuckled.

"But Amma and Affa won't let me."

"Is that a warning?" asked Fleer, raising a jagged mountain ridge of scales above one milky eye. "Come," he said. "I'll choose to ignore your warning. Let's tell them that we're going."

Roar wouldn't have dreamt it. Everything was too unimaginable. At a quarter to midnight by the moon, almost late, she and Gunkl Fleer arrived at the edge of the crowd. That was where she expected to stay, not being able to see or hear the concert. But a plump attendant dressed in a fake-scale jacket bustled forward and called out: "Here!"

A streamlined dragon-mover slewed over. "At last," snarled the driver. "Get in!"

The mountain loomed over them, black and jagged. The dragon-mover sped up the mountain, stopping at a rock-shelf just below the top.

Yet another overstuffed attendant opened the door beside Gunkl Fleer. "This way," said the attendant, gripping Fleer's scarred and wrinkled wing.

"Thank you, but Roar here will lead me," said Fleer.

So Roar touched Gunkl Fleer's wing lightly with her own as they followed. Roar worried that they had come too late. Row after row was full, and the attendant kept on walking. Finally, he found two seats side by side in the middle of the front row. After making sure that Roar and Fleer were seated, he blew a whistle and withdrew into the shadows.

Roar relaxed in her chair, relieved. "We almost didn't get seats," she said, "But everything's alright now." She looked up, and just ahead was the peak of the mountain, black against a dark blue sky.

Braah! went a horn.

Dwomp buh brrrrrrrah! went a drumroll, just like Talent Time. The audience went wild, over nothing. The only thing that sounded different compared to watching it at home was that here, Roar didn't hear the clicking of knitting needles. She choked back a schoolyard curse. Gunkl Fleer must have won two studio audience tickets, and didn't know the difference between Talent Time and a real concert, let alone C. Age had caught up to Fleer. He was just what Roar's parents called him in the privacy of the lair.

But a moment after feeling angry and ashamed of Fleer, Roar felt unaccountably tender for all those good times in the past. She leaned over and whispered in his ear, "Remember when—"

"Huff!" said Fleer, frying the air.

Then suddenly, another sound erupted, deep as if it came from the stomach of the mountain. It was as wide as the sky yawning, and bright as the sun. It made Roar's head jangle. It was the roar of a dragon. A *real* dragon, nothing reconstituted, nothing made up for the screen. Roar rubbed her ears, but the roar was still there, hovering in the air like a cloud of smoke, shimmering like a flame.

And now C leapt out of nowhere, to stand against the sky. He looked different now, like a new top of the mountain, a moving one, black and terrible and magnificently spiky against the ink-blue starry sky.

And now C roared in colour.

He snorted flames out of his nostrils. He spurted flames from his sword-toothed mouth. He roared and shook the mountain, and poured out fire that lit the sky—making thunder that rolled and then snapped—zigzagging fire-lightning. He whispered tiny huffs of smoke clouds that clothed him in a mist—and then he waved his wings and tore them into wisps. He poured out curlicued flagrations, and waved his head and contorted his mouth, and out came fire-paintings— great fighting monsters of Old, poised to leap upon him. And he played with them, balancing one on a wing, tossing it onto an elbow, then dropping it and stamping it squished with one foot. He stabbed another monster with a flick of his talons, and smithereened another with a snap of his bristling tail.

Sometimes C painted with fire so silently that sounds squirmed in Roar's earwax. And then C roared so earshakingly that pictures jiggled in Roar's eyeball juice.

And all the time, C moved blackly so that whichever way he stood, he looked magnificent but mysterious—wild, unapproachable, not of this time and world.

"See," the crowd shrieked. "See see see!"

Then he painted a flaming ship with little salties leaping from it, and the crowd screeched, "Sea sea sea!" Or anyway, that is what Roar screeched with them. By that time, Roar had shrieked and screeched and yelled so much that she lost her breath.

Finally, C slashed the air with a sweep of his claws, waved his wings with a swooshing flap, filled his mighty chest with one humongously long deep snort—and threw out the longest and most curlicued flame of all—this time, of a flame-red, wide-headed, flat-faced wingless dragon that looped like a giant serpent.

"It's her!" screamed Roar into Fleer's ear.

And the dragon that C painted danced in the air, as delicately as a falling blossom, as lithely as a flame.

And from a sound of the crowd that Roar had had to scream over, to try and still fail to be heard, there grew the sound of four thousand nine-hundred and ninety-nine dragons (all the audience except Gunkl Fleer) holding their breaths.

And then she evaporated, to be lost to the night, just as all of C's amazing pictures.

"No wonder you loved her," Roar sighed. "I wish you could see."

Roar turned to Fleer, but already had to scream into his ear. "Oh, Gunkl. I'd give anything for you to have seen."

Fleer patted Roar's hand, which had clutched his wing in a surprisingly strong grasp.

"I do see," Fleer said. "That's what memory is for."

Roar had to lip-read in all the noise, to understand, but she did. And she also saw an unusual trail catch the light in a zigzag amongst the scales from Fleer's left eye, all the way down to his chin.

"Don't want to miss the show," he said, turning to the stage.

C was doing his last encore—a showy starburst of flames.

And then C dropped below the peak to disappear. The sound of one last roar rumbled to nothing, lost in the cries of the crowd.

Gunkl Fleer leaned towards Roar. "This was probably bad for you."

"Yes," grinned Roar, but she had yelled so much her chest hurt. "I wish... you could..."

"Breathe in and out in little sips," said the ancient dragon. "Ah. Hah."

"Ah. Hah."

"Keep going," said Gunkl Fleer.

"Ah. Hah. Ah. Hah."

"Good. What's that smell you're making?"

"I don't know," said Roar.

"Open your eyes."

"It's smoke!"

"Ahh," said Gunkl Fleer. "Your first huff. Our secret?"

Roar could hardly believe her eyes, so she rubbed them. Before she had a chance to open them again, a curled claw lightly scratched her knee. "Stay here," said Fleer.

"I wasn't going anywhere," said Roar, a bit hurt that Gunkl Fleer had so quickly forgotten this amazing event—Roar being able to puff smoke.

"Wait till everyone has left," said Fleer. "And then we'll go."

Roar dreaded the trip down the mountain. All that attention earlier, but now she and her ancient crippled gunkl were forgotten. Everyone was leaving, a few on foot till they got to the bottom with its parking lot, but most in dragon-movers from their places where they had watched—for who walked anywhere any more except for Gunkl Fleer? Roar didn't know how long it would take to guide Fleer home, but it would be at least all night. She wished she had enough money for a dragon-mover trip, but she didn't, and she'd never seen Gunkl Fleer spend money.

"Oh well," Roar thought. "He must have asked for help because of his age, but forgot to ask for help both ways." She sighed. "I guess I'll never be able to huff again, either."

"Patience," Fleer chuckled, "is often an excuse for laziness."

But Roar wasn't listening. She had closed her eyes to relive the best night of her life...

"Master!"

"Mischief maker!"

Roar's eyes sprang open. There in front of her, his great spiked head carving out a piece of the sky, stood C, wreathed in smoke. He was bowing to Gunkl Fleer, and grinning.

"And you must be Roar," said C.

Roar nodded. She couldn't think of a word to say.

C laughed. It started out small, and ended big. It started out all by himself, but was followed by the laugh of Gunkl Fleer, so that soon the Mountain reverberated with their laughter, for they were all alone on it—C and Gunkl Fleer, and Roar.

When at last, C and Fleer were finished laughing, C said, "Shall we go?"

"By the old means!" cried Fleer.

And with a sweep of his arm, C scooped up Roar and leapt in the air. He flapped once, twice, and the mountain slipped away from under them.

"Gungk—!" Roar was so mixed up, she couldn't have told you if that meant:

Gunkl, look at me (which would have been silly to say)

or

What a long way to fall

She looked down, terrified and thrilled as they cleaved the air. All her dreams were not as good as this moment rising toward the moon, but she felt sick inside.

"I have to go back," she said. "My gunkl can't see."

"I doesn't need to,"—and there was Gunkl Fleer, flying alongside, the slow flap of his wings being the exact same sound as—

Roar's heart jumped into her mouth, and she almost exploded. "You're not a fan!"

"Not when I last sniffed," laughed Fleer. "Slow down for an old dragon."

Just when they were far away, C and Fleer landed, halfway up another mountain.

"Welcome to my home," said C.

"Where?" Roar looked up and down the mountain, looking for the mansion lair of a star.

"Here," said C. He led through a crack that opened out

to a cave no bigger than Gunkl Fleer's. It also leaked.

C's home also had a few curiosities, not as big a collection as Gunkl Fleer's but enough that Roar was even more confused.

"She doesn't want to eat cardoons," said Fleer.

"Gunkl," Roar was so embarrassed, she wished she could slither out the crack.

"But she huffed tonight," said Fleer.

Roar didn't know what to say. She was ashamed and proud and confused, and surprised by everything all at the same time.

"Did you ever wonder about my name?" asked C.

"Everyone does," Roar said.

"I'm called C," C said sadly, "because they said I couldn't admit my real name."

"You?"

"My managers."

"But that's the past now," Fleer said in a tone that was a command. "Meet Cardoon," said Fleer.

"Cardoon!" said Roar.

"Roariferex," said Gregigk Ggidskxidg Undgkl Fleer, "Close your mouth or you'll swallow bats."

And the night continued far into day, and they still had so much to talk about.

"Those cardoons they grow and shove into cans really are disgusting," said Cardoon, who insisted on being called plain C in such intimate company, as C is easier than Cardoon, especially when talking about cardoons.

"They have made them grow all puny and stringy, the easier to boil them and can them. But come dawn, we'll fly to where cardoons grow wild and free—and you'll see that they are what made me, well... me!"

"And me," said Fleer modestly. "With a little this and that."

"Your Gunkl Fleer hasn't let this world know of his power."

"And I wasn't planning to yet. Not till you were old enough," said Fleer. "You pushed the time forward."

When dawn purpled the sky they flew out, this time with Roar asking to be held by Fleer, who was slow and steady in the sky and who used his nose like other modern dragons use their eyes.

They travelled over real villages and fields of sheep, where C and Fleer swooped down, plucking up, here a milkmaid, there a shepherd. "Try this," they'd say, tearing a head or leg off and offering the morsels to an astounded Roar.

They hovered over a cargo ship and tore the captain from his cabin.

"Not as good as the old salties," said Fleer.

"I wish I'd tasted them," said C.

Eventually they hovered over a field. It was not like a normal field or forest. This was green and blue and glints of silver, and it had a wonderful glitter, as though everything in it was made of points. And the field was dotted with fat spots of the colour of jewels of Old—purple topaz streaked with shining black.

"Now!" yelled C and Fleer together.

"Pick up your feet, Roar," said Fleer, but not fast enough, for as he swooped and plucked a graspful of cardoons from the field, "Yow!"—Roar's legs were slashed by a thousand little swords.

"That'll teach you," laughed C. "I've got the scars, too, from before I toughened up."

They landed on another mountain, where C and Fleer taught Roar the way to eat cardoons.

You hold a stalk in your talons. You need the thickened skin of your feet for what's to come next.

Now you cook it with a quick breath. Don't breathe too long or too hard, or you'll burn the cardoon right up. It should just toast. And then you eat it. The spiky spiny leaves—sharp and pointed like a handful of knives—now curl and go all crispy, each edge and spine and spike leaking a curl of smoke. Their former sharpness now makes the tongue tingle just right, and when you crunch, they shatter between your teeth. There's nothing smelliverous about a wild cardoon, or slimy or anything faintly resembling that stuff that they pack in cans.

These didn't look or taste like dead frogs, and they weren't puny either. They looked magnificent—standing taller than a man. They weren't a boiled colour, but what Roar would never have dreamed... blue and green, streaked with gold.

Fleer picked up Roar and they flew on with C at their side, picking a bit of this and that.

"Now this is a balanced diet," declared Fleer, "with shreds you can suck from your teeth."

Roar nodded because her mouth was full. She'd just been given a scrap of woodsman by one of Fleer's feet, and with the other, a toasted cardoon leaf. They were now over another cardoon field, this one even more colourful.

"Pick her a head," said C. "She can look at it."

"Good idea," said Fleer, He circled over the field, sniffing, and swooped on one of the round splashes of purple topaz streaked with black. Roar heard a mouthwatering snap.

"That's what Vikings sounded like," said Gunkl Fleer. "Take this."

It was a cardoon head, and it smelt droolicious but it looked even better. Huge sharp scales that refused to stay flat. They shined blue and green with streaks of gold. On the top of its head, a kind of flower burst out, purple topaz streaked with black. It didn't look cannable. It didn't look boilable. It looked like it could fight monsters, and win.

"You can't eat it yet," said Fleer, "but your tongue will know it soon."

Roar looked at C, and suddenly knew.

Cardoon looks like cardoons!

Roar was having a hard time eating, even though it all

made her saliva run. But her jaws had never worked before. She'd never eaten anything that needed chewing. She'd never before *seen* food that needed serious chewing. Everyone thought it too much work.

"Your teeth hurt," said C. "Mine did too at first, but we'll keep them."

Finally they stopped in a valley. "Just beyond is a city," said Fleer. "Do you think you're ready?" he said to C.

"What do you think, Roariferex?" asked the dragon whose full name is Cardoon.

Roar didn't know what to think, so she did the next best thing. "Gunkl Fleer says that patience is an excuse for laziness."

"That's a good enough excuse for me." And to Roar's surprise and terror and thrill, they flew to the city and snatched up office workers from offices, laptop-tappers from their beds, couriers from their bicycles, Hells Angels from their motorcycles, screen watchers from everywhere. They flew over a beach so they could snack saltily, and opened up a movie house so they could pick up some snack-filled children. And before they were full, they flew off, the sweet sound of a city's screaming trailing them like ribbons in the wind.

They ended up at C's place, where they did some more explaining.

"You had a much easier time eating the city people, didn't you?" said Fleer.

"They didn't need half as much chewing," agreed Roar.

"They're still better than Milkmaids and Salties," said C, "which reminds me."

He walked off and came back with a box of each, opened. He offered them to Gunkl Fleer, who sniffed and took two Salties and a Milkmaid.

"Droolicious," said Fleer.

"Have some," said C, offering the boxes to Roar.

Roar could have been turned to rock. She couldn't

believe her eyes.

"She's frightened of them," said Fleer.

"I'm not frightened of anything," said Roar before she could help herself.

"You should be," laughed C. "These'll rot your teeth out if they're the only things you eat. But—"

"Moderation." said Fleer. "A bit of this and that."

"That's what you taught me," smiled C, though Fleer couldn't see.

So, before Roar fell asleep, exhausted, she learned even more things.

That Gunkl Fleer had noticed C on his travels—a starving, neglected young dragon wandering on the edge of a crumbling city. That Gunkl Fleer had taught C everything needed to live, but that Gunkl Fleer and C had both needed to be independent. At least that was what they said.

They also said that even Roar's parents could learn how to fly, if they stopped sitting and did some exercise. Sure they'd fly in circles because of those bent tails, but circling is better than nothing.

Then they told Roar how C had invented a simple elastic band that grown-ups like Roar's parents could use to keep their false teeth in, so that they could pluck up softies (that's what C and Fleer call city people).

They said, and then they swore, that any dragon, with practice, can learn to not only huff, but roar and spout flames (though painting with flames is a talent that takes exceptional practice, dedication, skill and talent).

But by the time they were almost finished telling, Roar's mind had wandered back—back to C's invention. Roar flicked her tail back and forth and closed her eyes.

"She's had too much today," Fleer and C agreed, and began to talk together of the old times, before civilisation wreaked bottoms on dragons.

By the time Roar flew home, not always being held by

Cardoon or Gunkl Fleer, she was ready to tear the poster from her bedlair wall because she could never imagine wanting to live in a lair complex again. She loved the feel of wind on her wings, the way the air combed the rising scales on the top of her head. She loved to flare her nostrils at the scent of water falling from rock. She thrilled to sniff the smell of fear in a fresh-plucked snack. She loved looking back at herself as she flew, and watching the way the scales on her back caught the sun (and the moon!) now that she was living a healthy outdoor life.

She had new secrets, too.

In this world, Roar learned, *there are only rare places where real milkmaids live, and woodsmen and shepherds.* She kept the secrets of Fleer and C, so that these places could live on. *Plucked lightly, and occasionally, there will be milkmaids and shepherds as forever as dragons, if they are not harvested without care.* That was what happened to the salties on the sailing ships. All gone, as gone as those old ships. Fleer and C showed Roar villages that they'd camouflaged with nets that sprouted with what looked like real cardoon factories and factory fields of stunted plants the colour of dead frogs. The nets even sprouted those advertising signs bragging of the way these cardoons will make you grow "in 12 different ways".

"When dragons fly again," said Fleer, "they'll fly over this as fast as they can."

And they all three laughed at their secret.

By the time Roar flew home, she was missing her parents fiercely. Of course, they knew that Gunkl Fleer had taken their little one someplace special and that she would be gone for a while, and they had hoped that Gunkl Fleer wasn't old and silly, but old and wise.

So when Roar got home, there was a celebration to beat all others in the Glak household, even though—when Mrs. Glak opened the door not only to her dear Wiwi and Gunkl Fleer, but to... *oh!* she fainted.

There was so much everyone had to say, and so many promises made. And in the spirit of all this honesty, there were even some confessions.

Roar confessed that she had been worried that Amma and Affa would die from eating Milkmaids and Salties, because she believed the WARNINGs on the boxes too much.

Mr. Glak confessed that he LOVED the idea of wearing knitted creations made by his beloved Flagration, but that he HATED wearing them. "I have sensitive skin," he said, lifting his sweater up. "The porcupines itch."

"I'm so sorry," said Mrs. Glak. "I tried to make the sweaters to fit your handsome, rugged look."

"Me? Rugged?" He lifted his shoulders from their slump.

She rushed to tear the sweater over his head and off his back, and narrowly missed his left eye with a giraffe hoof, or maybe it was a sheep's horn.

But what surprised all of them the most was Cardoon's confession.

"I wish I belonged to a family."

"You do!" said Roariferex, Flagration, and Terrorfik Glak, all at the same time.

Gunkl Fleer smiled, but now that Roar had developed her senses a bit more, she thought he smelt a little sad.

"Gunkl Fleer hasn't confessed anything."

"What do I have to confess?" said the ancient dragon.

"You know," said Roar. "I can't reveal your secrets."

"There's a lesson to you," said Roar's father, running a hand over his now naked belly.

Everyone was quiet, and they stayed quiet till Gunkl Fleer huffed once, a gentle sound that pushed a small cloud into the air.

"Would you like some help?" asked Roar.

"I don't know where to start," said Gunkl Fleer. "So yes."

"We'll start with a question," said Roar, imitating Gunkl Fleer's own teaching style. "Why did you lose your love?"

"Love?" broke in Flagration Glak, clasping her wings to

her chest, her eyes glowing.

"Shh," said Terrorfik, reaching for her.

"I lost my love," said Gunkl Fleer, "because she always had a line of people who came to her for their good fortune. Back in those days I could see around the world and up my own back to the top of my head, and the line of people who came to her was almost that long."

"And she didn't eat them up?" said Terrorfik Glak.

"Oh, I wanted to! But her kind doesn't eat people. Her kind of dragon does good things for people. I really don't know why, but that's as they are made. The only people she considered right to eat are bad people, but who can decide that?"

Everyone gasped except for Roar.

"So we could never be together," said Gunkl Fleer, "Even if you had accepted her."

"She makes Dragonair look like a dead frog," said Roar.

Gunkl Fleer's hard eyebrows rose, and fell. "That's the past," he said. "Centuries ago."

"I've seen her," said Cardoon quietly. "She misses you, too."

But Terrorfik Glak had not been listening.

"You mean those boxes really scared you?"

"No Affa. I was happy reading how you'd die, and looking at those pictures. The closeups of blue-eye, hooknose, a gangyellowed jaw. Why didn't they scare you?"

"They're ugly. I turned them—"

"My way."

Flagration Glak uttered a low growl. "The Curlopsis Council has a lot to answer for. I shall write them a stinging letter."

"No, Flagra." Terrorfik tore off his gloves and raised his puny fists. "No one wrote letters in the old days. A fear for a fear, I say."

"Oh, Affa!" Roar laughed, wanting to curse. "That's just

a theme song."

"Not quite," said Fleer. "Ee fleerrr frr ee fleerrr. That is the Old Code."

"Fleerrr?" everyone said with various capabilities (Mrs. and Mrs. Glak having to turn around to reinsert their dentures).

"Everything's too easy on the mouth these days," grinned Fleer. "A fear for a fear it shall be."

"Their lairquarters is a short ride away," said Flagration. "And oh!" She rushed to the kitchen and came back brandishing a can of cardoons. "See?" she demanded.

Everyone looked at the big Circle of Recommendation from the Curlopsis Council, and the sudden air-fry from several mouths caused the temperature-constant on the air-con to whir itself to death.

"No more of these," Flagration Glak declared, shaking the cardoon can. "And no more boxes. From now on, I'll throw all the Milkmaids and Salties into serving bowls. But, dear," she said to Terrorfik. "How will you serve the Council a fear for a fear?"

He hung his head. "I can't, but perhaps Fleer and C—"

"Patience," said C. "And we'll make it a family outing." He turned to Fleer. "As I was saying, I've seen her…"

And now, so much has changed.

These days Gunkl Fleer and his great love (who has a name everyone delights in, as it tickles the tongue) travel far and high together. Sometimes she carries Fleer on her back as she races over sea and land—and sometimes she is coiled around Fleer's scarred but wiry body as he flies. And sometimes they fly with the rest of the Glak family (who can now swoop right or left or divebomb straight as an arrow, due to the Roar Flying CrookTail Service which provides all needy adults—which means pretty much all grownups—with training and the Roariferex Tailbase Corrector, *now with knitted anti-chafing pads*). But that's a diversion, so let's get back to

Gunkl Fleer and his love.

Sometimes they fly quite alone—just the two of them—out to find new wilderness. And they live by their new agreement: Whenever they stop and a line of people forms to ask her to do good things for them, Fleer and his love eat only every third person.

And now when no one eats canned cardoons any more, all those still, silent, stunted fields meant for the boilers have grown wilder and freer than ever before, and spread. Muscled leaves unfold, relaxing talons. Great heads rear up, flashing gold and topaz spikes. So, reader, heed this WARNING. Eat your vegetables, or choke them to death, or teach them to fly away, or dress them in something so craftily knitted that they scratch themselves to death. Everyone is droolicious to someone else. *We are Cardoons! We not only scratch. We bite. Hear us, Roar!*

I KILLED
FOR A LUCKY STRIKE

... so that bullet meant for someone else tore through his windpipe.

Yeah, it's ironic but effective as being froze in hell. Anyway, Death flew in fueled by years of anticipation. But instead of a gloriously antiheroic End fit for Death's collection, blood was leaping from the man's throat like rats from any old doomed place. And those famous piercing eyes? They were just blanks. You'll live, said Death, plugging the hole with a dirty sock. Hey, shouted Life. You think I want this guy? Pick him up! But Death had split.

Yes, that's the end of that one, sir. You enjoy all that? Glory be, just look out the window. Ain't that the most gorgeous golden sun? You could use some, but it's setting now. How's about something sweet? You look like you need it after all that icky stuff you've chucked down.

Yes, bitter things do need sophistication to appreciate. But come on, admit it. You can't not want pie. Now, I'd love to be able to eat cherry pie but—No? You want the check? Another cuppa Joe? No?

Sir, please *remove* your hand and wrap it around your coffee cup. Yes indeed I mean it. So if you don't want—

Yes, sir. If you say I can't take a bit of friendly play, you must be right. The cash register's over—huh? So I've just ruined your day? Sir, just letting you sit there makes this your lucky day. Accountants!

What? You're *not* an accountant? Well, slap me cold. I'm just a dumb piece who didn't add up the notebook in your breast pocket, your corduroy jacket and the need to protect your elbows with cute leather patches. An accountant spends too much time at a desk, just like you, but he doesn't have time for words. He lives dangerously. An accountant, sir, always has to watch his front.

No, I don't have a thing about them. Well, that's very gracious. I accept your apology. You'd like more? What, precisely? Not if you keep looking at me like that. Besides, no offense, but you're like a dog judging Miss America. Sure I'm a stunner, but my vital statistics are a waste on you. Been a pleasure. Here's the check. Come again sometime (the week after hell freezes over). Who? Yes, that's my boss.

You can't want another serving. Seriously? Please, sir, take my advice: Noir is not healthy. And the Noir Special you asked the boss to say yes to—it's *more* unhealthy. Of course you are, and I'm just the—I *do* understand. You're the orderer, I'm the order taker. No, I *don't* care. It's *your funeral.*

So how about my early years? I remember when I was born. Noise. Lights. The smell of oil, my first quick dip, the thorough toweling, tagging, wrapping up. I think everyone spoke Spanish. I remember there were cork trees, the crunch of leaves, bright sun beating down on me till I was so hot some handler dropped me. I remember the smell of wicker, greased paper, donkeys—

Nope, I'm not playing with you. I just thought something sweet—

Then it's night, of course. A few unbroken soda lights barely illuminate a street running with vomited liquor made of wood scraps and other fermentables, rats skittering to flee food baggers, and rain—a steady drizzle as relentless as a protection collector. There's a terrifying taint of rust in the air, acidified to the breaking point by lashings of hoarse, hopeless laughter. It's Frankfurt, 1921 or so, since you want something personal. Could be that's where I was born. Anyway, I've just been traded for a loaf of bread.

I distinctly remember that both sides of the trade were, by the next day, as unhappy as a wet neck. As you've seen, I've got good lines, great nose, distinguishment. But so much of my life, I've been just a piece. Good lines don't matter. You can write that down. Just like, but you already must know this line: *Very few things happen at the right time, and the rest do not happen at all.* So doesn't it crack you up as it does, me, that Herodotus is *said* to have said it, but only Twain said he said it, and Twain only made it up? Isn't that the kind of story you'd rather have?

No was enough. *Hell* was overkill. Just what, precisely, do you want?

Men? How they had me? Forget it, but men who've had me, you can have.

Before he had a shtick (if you don't know what I mean, you can raise your hand) Ivor Gufferlund picked me up at Caesar's Palace. That day, he still said *acrost* for across, like every hick his side of Iowa. But he'd served his country for three long years, broadening his mind and expanding his horizons as he dug roads for the Iowa State Department of Corrections.

A man like him wasn't meant for growing corn, so instead, he'd become a salesman, selling crop insurance for Prairie Pride, a company he'd established in his head. He learned two lessons from that time. Location location location, and time time time. He really should have left Iowa if he didn't want to chance selling to his Ma's second cousin's Poppa. And as a businessman, he certainly should have known when enough was enough.

The day I met him, he was like a baby, fresh-released, fresh off the Greyhound bus, wearing the clothes he'd been arrested in—neatly patched bib overalls. They'd made such a good impression, those and his honest blue eyes.

As I said (but will tell you once again because of your corroded memory) Gufferlund picked me up in Caesar's Palace. I was behind the lefthand bank of slots, in the middle stall of the Men's. He walked in, first place he went to off the bus. He was busting for a crap, so naturally wanted his first dump to be somewhere indicative of his new direction. Men are superstitious, so he didn't consider any other stall. He pushed it open and shut it behind him, almost stepping on me as he did. Sitting on the can was J.B. Livesay, his big white head holed like a Lifesaver—and he sure didn't smell like mint.

I could hear from Gufferlund's gulp that this was his first dead man. But his recoil was admirable. He rifled Livesay's pink satin jacket pockets and then—and only some would think to do this—Ivor Gufferlund reached down and fumbled with Livesay's pants—and fast as you can say *slip*, I was his.

And I don't remember his name, but I was with this other guy at some wedding where there was a lot of celebrating, lots of fireworks going off in all calibers, and he was prone to migraines. He was standing around waiting till he could leave without offending when the guy next to him, who hadn't shot off a round, produced a Lucky Strike and proceeded to light it. My man, who was a hypochondriac 4-pack-a-dayer of Camels, had been trying to quit so he hadn't had a decent pull for a week.

That this guy next to him had such bad etiquette to not celebrate was bad enough, but the column of smoke sidling by my guy's nostrils was too much for his willpower.

Gimme that, he says. Why? says the rude smoker. My man put me to work so fast, by the time stupid's head hit the concrete, not only had my guy snatched the Lucky, but tossed it in disgust. Oh, that's right. He was known as The Evaporator. He sidestepped so smoothly, he would've got away with it, but he dumped me in a vase of roses and baby's breath.

The next guy who picked me up was Leonardo "Lilies" Gambaragno. He was as much 'my man' as they all were. He left with the vase of flowers, being very fond of vases of fresh flowers. A week later, Lilies was horrified when he pulled me out. He never understood me, but he kept me oiled. Lilies had qualities, but he was an addict. Never steal a vase of flowers from the fresh grave of your boss's Mama.

So what's wrong now? Don't say "nothing". You look like a stopped sink. Isn't this what you ordered? "Almost" isn't English. You *say* just keep going, but I can smell your sweat. A little exposé of my life here—what it feels like to serve you? The boss sell you this? I bet you teach Ulysses but read it for the panty scenes. You want me to talk dirty, you can have that. *Raw*, is it? Say! You gotta publish or perish, don't you? So how about I do you a nice big "Incidences of exsanguinated exits: Is nihilism mere naïveté in disgui—

Now, why would I want to play with you? I just thought—

Yup. Sir, please lower your voice. What? Yes, I *do* know you could have me fucking fired.

Here's your *raw*, gutter fresh.

First of all, I like someone I can't trust. They're dependable.

More than one man has patted me and given me the treatment, the old *my only friend, the only one I trust.* But when it comes right down to it, what did I tell you? To some of them, I might as well have been a piece of kleenex. *Use it and lose it.*

No one knows a man like his closest companion. His clothes make you, not him, if you think they tell you more than precisely: nix.

It's the scent of a man, *that* is the man. Down where I've been—some I've wished I could slip my safety, and just go *Bam!* Hm? You? You're fine. Yes, better than fine. Looks? Sure they matter. You? Turn your head. I'd say like a Cary Grant, with more depth of course. Yes, you are exceptional.

Types? Gosh. For every kraut whose outer garb is spotless

and whose underwear hasn't been washed for a month, there's another who's so clean, he could fake his trail by adding wheels to a bar of Lifebuoy. And I should know. I've been with kikes, spics, wops, micks, dagos, hunkies, crackers, a couple of fratboys, one professor; men of more colors than an opened corpse (*you* get your kicks rollin that n-word around your mouth). Judges and cops of course, and enough holy men for about 66 percent of a stale joke.

I've traveled all classes including stow-away, been holed up in dives, been with men taking walks on beaches till long past sunset; done huge slabs of time doing nothing but waiting, listening to the seltzer bottle spritz, ice cubes clink, teeth clinking against glass, glass crashing into teeth; I've spent time in libraries, public and personal; been to operas where I could feel his tux shaking to the spasms of my man of the moment's silent sobbing; been to clubs where the music throbbed and the air was thick with inarticulate boasts and threats, sometimes punctuated by cordite. Yeah, often I was put to work when I wanted only to listen, to watch, to rattle and roll like a drop of sweat on a plugged man's gizzard.

Not that I got the choice. I was just an instrument of desire, a tool in any man's hand who had me. And more have had me than I care to count.

Mmm.

Pino Conivino. I didn't know him before he transformed himself, but he had been your typical smart fat Jewboy whose father expects him to be a doctor. So he ran away from home some fine Sabbath while his mother was washing chicken fat off dishes, found work in Newark humping pig carcasses for an eyetie butcher, and soon found that the crafty little wop was using him as a courier to transport something illegal in those pigs. (I don't know what, honest.) By the time Pinchus Cohen had wised up, he'd transformed himself into a fine specimen of a man—a regular God in the Looks Department. He was honey to the dames. And he was a target, since he too obviously had begun to think for himself.

That's when he picked me up and took me to Atlantic City. He was okay, Pino was. Sure, he changed his persona as etiquette demands. He was Pinchus Cohen to his new wife and later, his kids. He was a valued pallbearer in his synagogue. And to his girlfriends, he was both generous and either Pino or Pinchus, depending on their needs. To me he was truly faithful till the day he died—from a heart attack says the death report, simple, and that is true, but I was sitting on the night table next to him when into the room comes, like some tipped-off Moses: his wife.

Mostly, I've been bounced around, sometimes treated like a trophy or a toy, often like a toothpick. It wasn't my choosing. Think what you like. Why should I care? In fact, if you hadn't noticed, this patois is for you.

Howsabout a lovely tale in Japanese, Yiddish, or Cantonese? Or a nice lot of limericks? Hey, like a little Lear?

Fuck. Bleakness had bled dry, clogging gutters with its clotted ennui. Nothing matters. Meanwhile, the tiniest nothing matters because, you know. Choices choices cho—

No need to get shirty. Much ado about nothing.

Jereboah McClure—quite the soprano. Killing used to bring out the *Ave Maria* in him.

Jerzy Lenchinsky—big on peaches and vodka. Very forgetful when drunk. One hot summer night in Chicago, absentmindedly shoved a peach in my face, mashing it in till it went up my nose. I never trusted him after that, but then I hadn't trusted him before, so I was even. We didn't last long. He slipped while climbing up a fire escape.

Professor Constantine Christophelus—a gentleman and a scholar. Unfortunately, he knew too much. Would you like a tidbit of classical Greek?

"Sweet J" P.J. Purdey—I would have loved to kill him, but I didn't get the pleasure.

I've had so many, they tend to bleed into each other. You'd probably list it as obsession, but cleanliness means so much. A clean man, even someone like "Barracuda"

Testerman, always thinks not simply of himself. Clean men paid me attention. They kept me well oiled.

Sadists, however, are something else. I've seen many, killed some.

Who have I killed?

Shouldn't you be asking if I had a choice? They were all rats.

The ones that got news coverage were all what nice people think of as dirty rats, but some of them were nice, and most of them were clean-shaven. If I were some lawman, they would quote me: "They might have been nice but they were no good."

No, I've never been bagged, never dragged into court. But I've spent too much time with the smell of dust frying on dirty radiators, healthy sexually aroused cockroaches, unwashed tooth glasses browned with whisky scurf. I've spent too many nights clutched in a sweaty paw.

I could design—from layered memories of the deep stench of failure—a spray repellent called Pawn Shop.

I could write of the boredom, frustration, infuriosity of enforced companionship, of being secreted in so many repellent places.

I *could* tell you, intimately, of my Life. Not that I trust you.

But *hell*, maybe that's why I *should*.

Am I your first Mauser? Oh, I know what. You must wanna know about flies. Having been with so many men in the profession, I've known a lot of flies. Some men, they are forgetful, and some like to souvenir.

Flies are inevitable. More than once, I've been witness to their whole life cycle, from them squirming around like little swaddled John and Mary Does, to them as adults doing their Magnificent Flying Trapeze act.

I used to wish I had legs, a heart, etc., but then I realized, after many men who didn't do better with all that stuff, that I am a damn sight better off without the fripperies. No stumbles, no heart attacks, no outrageous sights I could make of myself, like Jereboah McClure as a lunch guest in Nick Riggio's, not realizing he should have ordered a steak because cutting his spaghetti was, to Riggio, a mortal insult. If only McClure had sung *Ave Maria*, but he wouldn't have because he wasn't planning on killing anyone at that lunch, and didn't think to sing to live.

But you must want to know about flies.

Because of our relative life expectancies, I got to know so many flies, they were hard to name. I started out, naturally, with Looey, but before I knew it, Looey the Fourteenth had died. By Looey the Fifteenth I lost interest. Maybe they even got me down. All that activity, just to live. To what purpose? We live to die. Quel noir, quel weird.

Cockroaches? I'm not going there. They often used to tickle me in the times when I've been well cared for. The reckless ones have gone up my nose where a few with perverted tastes have gnawed, but not for long. They leave soon, but their stench permeates.

Broads? As for broads, babes, dolls, dames, frails, chits, chicks and minxes, skirts and worse, I don't want to call them that. They're women to me, though some of them are ladies, but only the ones who'd never call themselves that. All the self-styled ladies I've seen are never that. Some are bitches, most are bags. Anyway, for years I wanted to be touched by a woman, but it didn't happen. Not only that, but from the ones I liked, I never got a sideways glance of like, though many of revulsion. What could I do? I yearned. Not for just any woman. Women aren't flies. I've seen enough to know. I started wanting someone, someone special.

Impossible, I know. Unreachable. Out of this world. *Screwball thought, ratkiller*, I said to myself. Didn't stop me thinking. Nothing could.

Of all the disgusting things that have happened to me including being shoved under unwashed armpits, into underpants smelling of a sewer—nothing has made me feel as unable to choose, to really change things—to say, haul off and do something—as when some guy silencers my kisser. Besides, dumb euphemism. It's like that mark who was 'terminated' at the Twirling Lariat in Bozeman, where you couldn't distinguish between a customer's ketchupped Western omelet and the ex-mark's head goo gore.

A silencer is a muffler at most to you, and a muzzle to me at best. Think about how you'd feel with some tube clamped on your breathing parts so you can hardly squeak or breathe, let alone spit, and you have to work faithfully, all so choking gasses can flood up your sinuses, trying to find their way to your hurt and pissed-off brain. And it doesn't even silence me. Anyone tuned right can hear me fine. *Give me* the dignity of choice? No guy would think of that.

Some haven't even cleaned me after I did their dirty work. *Bam, bam*, and they hock my ass. Being in a pawn shop is hell, but it gives you empathy and time to think. (Guitars, for instance, can give you so much empathy, you want to become a cold machine; of wedding rings, it's better not to think; but for soul-ripping empathy, there was one banged-up grave-diggers shovel…)

That reminds me of another guy, name of… can't remember. You couldn't have hocked *him*. He was unvaluable. But now I remember why I forgot him in the first place. He was such a nothing, he flatlined before developing a story arc.

Back to the silencer. I was with this guy, Jerry Altsingher. He had to leave the city of angels without a backwards glance or change of clothes, so he drove up the coast thinking to hole up someplace small—Oregon, then turn right. He stopped at a place along the Columbia River that had a restaurant, a bar, and looked plenty holey. But with his faithfulness to seersucker suits—that evening, first in the restaurant where the retired peach farmers all discussed by yelling across the room, and then after he left quickly, in a bar with the lumberjacks—Jerry realized he wouldn't blend.

He skedaddled, fleeing back to the safety of the coast road. Up he drove, getting tired and cranky. And just when despair threatened to set in, Jerry's face brightened. I could see (from the dashboard) a comforting (for Jerry) smog ahead. The smell approached us like a speeding bullet— a complex fugue, worse than cockroaches, worse than the scents of Jerry. He was smell-blind, so his smile was so big, his top denture wobbled. As he drove into the actual town, he farted with relief. Perfect, he said. Not to me, of course. But I knew what he was thinking. This place was big enough that no one would cock an eye at him, just unfriendly enough in a beaten-down way, that no one was looking to like anyone, or—most importantly—give him a second glance. Hell, no one would spend a first glance.

This place is so unproud of itself I don't think it has a town sign—it would just get beaten up.

And he chose right. The town has no tourists, no bars filled with happy lumberjacks wanting to toss Jerry just for the joie de vivre. It's not a place where a guy in a seersucker suit would get the same welcome as an outbreak of rust. That town is, quite simply, your perfect Noirville. Not that Jerry knew that. He only saw a place just perfect to hole up for a month or two.

He burrowed in.

No sir, Jerry isn't exactly *raw* yet, but—no, I don't have literary pretensions and should have known Jerry is just an American road tale. I thought he was at least picaresque. Yes, I see these could be seen as just a string of anecdotes but— Yes, *sir!* The customer is always right. I'll noir things up. It'll be easier now anyway, since it's pretty dark here now. If you haven't noticed, the boss has left, so it's just you and me.

John Ott. He was *born* noir. Say a billboard across the street from Our Lady of the Pure-As-Driven-Snow Convent showed John Ott holding a bazooka accompanied by the supplication: BUY. The convent would go into overdrive making almond cookies to sell or the nuns would go out to turn tricks—to buy bazookas.

John Ott was as handsome and dangerous as a snake. His lips were a thin blue line. His foremost particular skill was stillness. He could wait anywhere and be as unnoticeable as a No Parking sign. His second skill was speed, so, like many before him, he chose me since I was so dependable.

Ott was a sadist. When he was between jobs, he just loved being unnoticed, then shoving a guy so the guy doesn't know what hits him. Then Ott materializes to inches from the target's tonsils. "You shoved me," Ott says to the tonsils, not even bothering to look at the terrified guy's eyes. Then Ott kind of herds his prey while the poor piece of squirming humanity begs forgiveness. Ott only releases his mental hold (he never touched his victims) after the man has thoroughly disgraced himself.

He never touched drugs, booze, or women. One night when he was having a fun time, a woman walks up to him. "You don't need to act that way," she says.

That's all she says. And she just stands there.

Ott's mouth drops open so wide, I can smell his gingivitis. He's monosyllabic at the best of times. A guttural grunt comes from him.

He's pulling into himself, deeper than I've ever known, then fingering me smooth as ever. His recoil is lightning, straight to her forehead for the Lifesaver—the holey strike.

She would have fallen. She was supposed to. But I jammed.

And that's how I met her. Ott dropped me like I'd burnt him, and he *ran away*. She picked me up and took me home.

We lived together, just the two of us—I was her closest companion, but she never packed me, never carried.

She'd never *wanted* to shoot a gun. Had always hated them. But I'd saved her life, so she liked me but didn't trust me. A perfect match.

No, sir. I didn't mean to give you All's Well That Ends Well, but I don't want to say any more. I'm sorry it gave you a bad taste in your mouth. Yes, I suppose you should just take it. Swallow that story with the happy ending. But sir, you being you and all, I thought you'd love that story, the supposedly happy ending with you knowing it didn't end there, not when I am here—here and now with you. Have you considered, sir, whether you're perhaps too fucking lazy to sprinkle on imagination?

Whoa, professor! I admit to getting carried away, but it's taking it too far to say I exploded.

But how's this? Does it help to know I never could work again as I was born to? That I'm still jammed. Yes, really. Still jammed, yes, sir.

So what? So I even ruined *that?*

Yes, sir. More men:

Kelvin Watts. If Clark Gable looked in the mirror and wanted to die, this guy staring back at him could be why. If he'd been in the mob, they would have called him Cantaloupe. Pencilstub mustache, reflective cranium, and the physique of a sack of melons that fell off a truck. He'd linked up with Oscar Weiderman, a guy born to counterfeit, but with no incentive. (I know all this because Oscar picked me up in Chicago years before he met Watts while simultaneously hiding and compulsively engraving lightbulbs, just to keep his hand in, while working as a chicken sexer in upper state Wisconsin.)

Watts didn't know, and Oscar never told him, but Oscar was supposed to be dead. Although he looked semi-dead, and had about as much worldliness as an egg yolk, he was famous in certain circles, and would have been as sought after as a lost diamond. That's why he always carried. Like breathing, it was Oscar's basic survival tic.

Watts ran Oscar like a Cadillac. Watts had an optimism and spark that warmed Oscar to his untrusting little toes. Oscar thrived in the admiration and creativity that Watts exuded. And Oscar—being rather cynicized by experience, and thus bereft of boundless imagination—left all the thoughts and planning to the worldly Watts.

After seeing Oscar's secret lightbulb art and getting filled in with a compulsive display of talents, Watts planned the scam: stamps. Not your philatelic, coroner's, or official passport kind, but the kind little old ladies buy to send letters to their grandchildren, and complaints to the newspapers, etc.

Oscar was mesmerized by Watts and absolutely loved the job variety. His stamps were works of art, portraying in the finest detail: Beetles (that he invented), Great Composers (that he made up so he could portray different beard arrangements), Heroes of the West (marvelous bogusities). He worked from home while Watts traveled the backroads of Minnesota in an old Buick, selling stamps to general store/ post offices with the proviso that they keep his amazing discount for bulk with a bonus of a free packet of paper and envelopes under wraps.

He did a roaring trade, but with Oscar's talents, Watts was soon demoralized by the inability of backroads to provide immense wealth. Besides, he'd never been to Vegas. So they went into greenbacks. And not just your nickel and dime stuff. Kelvin Watts was done with that.

Watts drove them to Vegas in the Buick, almost searing their lungs when they opened the windows. So they were delayed in getting into their first casino by needing to check into a motel, the first they found, and each needing to take a shower and Watts, shamelessly, needing to stand buck naked in front of the rattletrap air conditioner. Just for a while. By the time Watts had Brylcreamed the nine long hairs on his dome, he was raring to go.

They walked out to—not the nearest casino, which was what Oscar was hoping—but all the way to Caesar's Palace. (On the walk, Oscar's nerves were jangling. Sure, Watts had mesmerised him and given him the most fun he'd ever had. But he couldn't just stay at home here. A motel is not a home, and he hated the sound of the air conditioner. Suddenly, he missed sexing chickens—just him getting personal with the chicks and no one looking at him sideways. And though I hadn't mentioned it before, he had caused quite a stir in upper state Wisconsin when he disappeared, for he had been the best chicken sexer they'd seen since Granville Owens, who died of feather allergy. Not that Oscar knew all that. He'd taken up chicken sexing only as a live-another-day job. All that, Oscar was thinking, and he almost turned and ran. But one look at Watts reassured him, and even thrilled him. Watts was as bright as a brooder's light.

Once in the refrigerated paradise of the Palace, Oscar (and I) felt a whole lot better. As you know, he wasn't the outgoing type, so he watched Watts from the slots while Watts went to get the chips.

How I wish you'd asked for alliterations, or better yet, puns. Or rhyme. It takes two to Camus. How's about Nietzsche is preachy? Not even Fart to Sartre? You *must* like Céline is mean. Well, he is. But I forgot. You like that—*mean*, I mean.

No, I'm not here to criticize you. And yes, since you ask—the story *does* have an ending.

Watts asked for quite a pile of chips, a whole three hundred bucks-worth. He handed over one of Oscar's beautiful bills, so neatly laundered, it was velvety with wear. That's when I found out the difficulties in spending a thousand dollar bill.

The scenario of Watts being hauled off didn't take but a moment to unfold before Oscar jerked like a guest in some electric chair. And he ran like I'd never known him to, weaving nimbly between the one-arm-bandits. Unfortunately he was recognized, and not by no fowl farmer.

He was neatly tripped so that he fell into a hefty someone's arms, who bundled him away before you could say *ricochet*. He was spirited to a private room where he was given an offer he could not refuse. In the course of the interview, it was made clear to him that he had overdressed. So he was relieved of the excess, of which I was a part.

That was how I ended up with the guy whose head was Lifesavered who I mentioned, remember, who Ivor Gufferlund—remember him? found. Small world.

No, I wasn't being sarcastic.

Now, haven't you had enough?

That wasn't noir? I don't believe this. You want *what?*

Me? You want the real stuff on me? How I felt when . . . oh, yeah.

I thought you were all Nietzsche, *all Alles, was tief ist, liebt die Maske.*

Don't tell me you don't know German.

French, Middle English, and Latin? Goddamn, I should have served you noir in Latin.

You're right again, sir. You didn't come here to get lectured at. Of course you'd know his line. I'm sure you teach it in the language of literature, English. *Everything deep loves a mask.* Of course you know. So, naturally, you being you and all, I thought you would not only love a mask, but expect it.

I don't believe this. Are you *crying?* Oh, baby, what's up with you?

So *what,* you've never killed anyone. I've never baked a cake.

You just wanna *touch* me? Did you see that on the menu? No, the boss would *not* have. Haven't you had enough? Look, it's your kind of bleak outside. Let's call it a—

A-plus, professor. I *knew* you could articulate if you had to. So you really want me to touch *you.* I guess I *could* make that a Special just for you . But how do I know I can trust you?

Geez, you do remember. *I only like someone I can't trust.* Word perfect. Just for that, I'll do you a special Special. Sit back, you handsome weird noirlover, and I'll do you good.

First, a little Frenching, then . . . ooh yeah, oh *yeah.* You *like* that, don't you? Don't try to talk, silly. You know you can't enunciate. Just open your eyes for me. I like to look at you. Whoa, baby! Better than noir, ain't it?

Well, I got a peep. Aren't you a flutterer. Baby, you sure are hungry. Thaass right, take it *all* in. You really *do* want it. Oooh, sugar! Oh, hoh, professor, I can smell your story arc developing. Just a little bit lon—hey, what I say about the hands?

I like you because I can't trust you? Oh, I do. I do.

I really really do!

(Oh, cherry pie. I really do think I'd love you.)

NONE SO SEEING
AS THOSE WHO'VE SEEN

I T'S the best of art, it's the worst of art, *Porn Eden*.

"The only surviving work by a hermit artist of unprecedented power, originality and technique, lost to history till discovered by one incredible woman," you would already know all about it. And if you can find what you've said, liked, shared, who you blocked because of it, you'd find so much.

Whole paragraphs, circa 2012 when some over-endowed one percenter or incredible forward-thinker or the Vatican or PETA nabbed the painting for what was then a record-shattering sum. Wise steal, fucking foolish spend, incredible blueprint, icon of the incredulous, altar upon which the misogynists of the world spurt their offerings. Woman's first bed upon which she draws her strength and inner disobedience. Work of God, work of the Devil. Or the most expensive paint stripper project in history—a spell wreaked on a rich idiot by fanatic makers movement activists—or, if the Sporangiophorians are right: the network that is us and the way we should reproduce if at peak of health—a mindbender that turns Watson and Crick's twist of DNA into a cocktail's twiddlestick.

Known: The artist didn't profit from the sale, being presumed, of course, dead.

Presumed known: Dead artists can't spend money.

Known known: Lucky for some.

But there are also known unknowns.

Alle vil vere herre, ingen vil bere sekken.
Everyone wants to be a gentleman;
nobody wants to carry the sack.

"I say, man," says Munch. "Nature! The soul."

Kvak nods, which gives him time to sift through the last few bits of nonsense to come out of Munch. This is the only way they've ever held a conversation. Munch proclaims, then exclaims. Kvak drinks and eats as much as he can get his hands on while Munch tosses profundities. And when necessary for response, Kvak sifts through the garbage of remembrance.

He lifts his empty glass in a solemn salute. Munch's cheek hollows are a mixture of carmine lake and orpiment, his thinly covered cheekbones Paris green.

"Nature also includes the inner pictures of the soul," says Munch, as if the idea's just come to him and he must reveal it. If you drink with Munch, you've got to put up with this.

Kvak always had before, but his back still hurts from yesterday's humiliating foray, showing *Eve's Couch* around. And Munch is only nursing a hangover from some salon last night where he was the center of attention though he's taken to repainting his most famous picture so much, he has turned into a self-forger.

Kvak looks sideways at Munch. He'd love to hurt him, but he doesn't know Munch well enough.

Instead, "Nature," he says. "But this soul you keep talking of."

Munch's head falls onto the sticky table, his shoulders shaking.

"See?" says Kvak. "There you go again. I keep telling you, you're too frail. You need to take better care of yourself. Are you laughing or crying?"

No answer except shaking shoulders and more

infuriatingly self-indulgent sounds.

Kvak slides off his chair onto the floor glittering with fish-scale sequins, blackened with the stuff tracked in on rope-soled sailor's shoes and hobnailed boots, greased from splashings of the tavern's rich and smelly soup. He puts his head sideways to eyeball Munch. "Edvard, you turn priests' hair grey, yet believe them? You think you have a soul?"

Munch picks up his head and straightens his back. His tidy little eyes, the eyes of a technocrat, sharpen to a point, his eyes darkly orbited by such unbearable sadness, they're Prussian blue. "I feel so *much*. Why this torture if I have no soul?"

The girl brings freshly filled glasses and waits, hands on aproned hips, for Munch to pay but even more so for Kvak to get off the floor and sit properly.

While he does, Munch reassembles himself till he looks merely like a melancholic visitor from the suburbs. He pays the girl enough that she leaves them alone again.

"You should get out more and talk with people," Kvak says. "If you met Americans, they'd tell you about soul. Maybe it's their scientific advancement. He got lotta soul, they say. They always say lotta when they talk about how much they have. And you know what lotta means?"

"Lotta," Munch says, curling his lip behind that mustache. Kvak can tell.

Munch. Kvak's hate for the man is now so pure, it burns in him with the purity of a spirit lamp—his feelings an invisible flame. He resents Munch, despises him for the contrast of their success—so much so that he wants to pull out a truth and wave it in the man's face. Kvak wants to tell Munch, *show Munch*, show him so clearly, there can be no misunderstanding. Kvak will show Munch the most beautiful thing—the discovery Kvak had seen with his own eyes once and now every single day, somewhere, in some back alley or on some bridge. The central truth of our being. "Do it now," he says. Why? In doing so, Kvak would lose his only thing of worth, this secret knowledge. In showing Munch, he'd show that he knows Munch to be a fraud. This would hurt them both irrevocably. But the hurt would be so pure.

He resents Munch so much that he has avoided seeing the man's success, so he has no idea that Munch has now taken to producing the kind of paintings people in the suburbs buy to complement their newly hung wallpaper.

Kvak sees only a famous man who uses him as an audience, and drinks with him to keep his little disgraces private.

"Let's go," says Kvak, pulling Munch up by the armpits.

Out they stroll, along the waterfront. And as luck would have it, within a hundred steps, a seaman is propped against a wall. His head is brown as a coconut, as is his neck down to a V. He's somehow lost his seaman's jacket and his vest. His shirt has been ripped open, exposing a chest as white as whalebone. His head is tipped back so the remaining of his few teeth show—brown as rotted piers. Mid-afternoon, so the shadows are falling fast, but the light was good enough. Good enough.

Kvak nudges Munch hard, and points.

"So?"

Munch's face darkens with annoyance. Kvak is a worm and a parasite. But he's been useful in getting Munch into a cab home, and he's never taken liberties to follow.

But the impertinence of the man! Munch shoves Kvak back so hard, Kvak reels across the street, stumbles on a scrap of rope, and falls with the peculiar grace of a drunk. Inexorably or not, his closely shorn skull strikes a bollard, waking the sleepy air. His mouth drops open.

Stark silently screaming sober, Munch runs away far as he can—far as he can—which was never, for the rest of his life as we know it— far enough.

Kvak's mouth hadn't dropped open. It was *pushed* open by a great cloud of stuff. If this was souls, it was an artist's souls. Great gobsy clouds of it. Munch's flee response was slowed by the paralysis of terror.

He was spattered, beaver hat to Italian leather shoes, with Prussian blue, cadmium yellow, chrome orange, viridian. A spat got into his tear duct. Because of dilution, he couldn't be sure of the pigment but thought it possibly madder lake. Even (and most dreadfully) his mouth did not escape. A big splat hit his lower lip, his tongue darting out and dragging it in before he could think. It stained his tongue and teeth black, but that wasn't the worst of it. The taste, that taste he would never forget: nauseatingly salty, tongue-burningly sour, so bitter he had attacks of retching for the rest of his life, one in which he had more time than he wished, to reflect. He'd never given Kvak credit, but this had to be Kvak's souls.

Munch only hoped no one saw *his* death. If he were lucky enough to die as Kvak, his souls bursting forth all the passions held within, he expected that he'd only puff pastels.

> *Barnesorg er snart sløkt.*
> A child's grief is soon put out.

Kjell Kvak got his first rattle when he was four years old. "Just as I told you," said his father, picking the boy up from his lap and setting him on the floor. "Nothing to be frightened of. And did you see the beautiful thing?"

"You must have been a great comfort." A woman the father had never seen before pushed between them and the bedside. "You say the *Fadervår* so beautifully. Uch!" she said, tugging at the old-fashioned, richly embroidered bodice that the dead woman's breasts no longer filled. "How embarrassing you are," she whispered at the body, her spit flying in its face, "All dressed up in your bridal finery. Good thing I'm the only sister to see this. No sense of *janteloven*. Always thought you were better than the rest of us. But you still died croaking like a crow caught in a pitchfork, eh. And your precious golden bridal crown. It didn't bring your husband back, nor one hair on your golden head, hah! Gold and bare as a magic goose's egg."

She shoved a flannel down her sister's open maw to shut off the staining dribble. "We can only hope He overlooks her sins," she said, looking over her shoulder to make eye contact with the pastor. But he had turned his son around and shepherded him from the room soon as she began her ministrations.

Father and son walked hand-in-hand away from that creaky old house with all its fanciful fretwork and delicate paintings making quite a heaven of the ceilings—to Pastor Kvak's apartment in a cobbled part of town, newer, more affluent, and much less romantic. Little Kjell sucked on a stick his father had given him—*brunost*, the cheese that tastes like caramel and that's so rich, it's meant to be served in a curl so thin, it's sliced with a wire.

The father chuckled quietly, thinking how Gustava would have carried on a storm. Gustava, the last of an unsatisfactory string of nursemaids, wouldn't have known how suchlike should be served. Only that no one should have it, let alone a child. She professed herself to be a strong pietist, as were many in the pastor's congregation. She declared a picture book he gave the child scandalous, as it wasn't the Bible. To keep the peace, the pastor reshelved the book, his childhood favorite, in his library. She was the type to declare buckwheat gruel and skimmed milk the only foods a child needs. What did the Pastor know about infant nutrition? So he made like a sheep once again (though he had stolen, at four years old, a feast of lingonberry jam and cold butter on hot *lefse*—and nothing bad had happened); Pastor Kvak gave way to Gustava as he didn't know where he'd find another.

The boy was so quiet and passive, his father rarely saw him. The child was so boring, so unknowable in his unquestioning gaze, that the father was slightly embarrassed on both their behalves.

Gustava had ruled in the nursery for three weeks when one sunny Saturday morning, with only the most perfunctory knock, she erupted into his library sanctum. After that she was more polite, almost delicate in her plea, nay, demand. "And I say again, it must be oilcloth. You might already be too late," she said. "But if you get it today, I can try to frighten the Devil away from him. But the horned one's worn a path to that boy. I'm sorry to say, sir, but you should have seen to it while the child was in swaddling."

"I never heard of a camp cot for a child. And you say all children are ruined if they sleep in a bed? I slept with my mother in that bed. They were the happiest hours of my life, so cozy and such sweet dreams. It closes off the world so beautifully—"

"Your mother was the key, don't you see? When a mother's away, the wicked do play." She took off her spectacles and touched a kerchief to her watery eyes. "The naughty boy makes water, sir. I can no longer hold back the truth from you. Dirtiness. I'm a poor woman, and the cost and trouble of needing another nightdress. I am not a laundress—"

"Yes, yes," said the pastor. "Tomorrow. Now let me work."

But any thoughts of writing a fresh sermon had flown out the door. They'd get a warmed up one, and (he sighed) most likely not know the difference. He picked his teeth with the steel tip of his pen. *My son, a bedwetter…*

Every half-past noon, Gustava took her charge out for an hour's walk, that day being no exception.

When they returned, she bustled the boy into the nursery with a series of grunts and chirps, something you might think of to herd a parrot who knew no Norsk. Above her vocals there was always a peculiarly irritating rasp, perfectly accompanying her jerky movements. How she could find a skirt that made you want to scream at its screeches—quite a talent.

A soft thud. Her hat being tossed onto a hook? As likely as she doing the can-can. But shh. She's talking. No. Whispering.

The pastor had to strain his ears to hear, but in his dead wife's wardrobe to which only he had the key, he could stand comfortably enough, his ear to the keyhole.

"… told you. Look all you like, you won't see him."

(the sound of a toddler starting to cry)

"Shush! Haven't I told you, your tears are the all the better to lick your face before he eats it."

(a small thud, and a floor board creaking)

"How many times do I have to tell you? Make a move and he can see you. Make a sound and he can hear you. He's nodding, he is. Don't you hear his neckbones creak? Listen. He says it's true. Open your mouth and whoosh! He'll see all the way down your throat. He can see into the places where your tears are made, and down the snailholes of your ears. He can see every bit of you and hear your every thought. And the *underjordiske* know it's true. They saw him come for you, his big forked toothpick in his belt. You think they're mice, don't you, the *underjordiske?*

"And if he can see and hear you, you must be a wicked little boy, for he's starving, having to live under that nasty bridge for all these years. Can't you hear him say it? Yes you should, for he doesn't waste words on himself. He's talking to you.

"*I am him what will not be denied,* he says. He's been starved for wicked little boys until he smelled you yesterday when we were out. And he followed your delicious wicked-ness, yum yum yum. And he climbed up into the window and unlatched it from the inside, and slipped past the flowers, and down to the floor, and then crept along the floor *right where you're sitting.* And he slipped up the wall while we were sleep-ing. If you'd only looked at the wallpaper you would have seen his glinting green eyes flashing this way and that, over everything as he slithers over the wallpaper, back and forth and up. And that streak there. See it? That's his drool. For today while we were out, can't you see?"

(no perceptible answer)

"Of course you can't. Only good children can see the troll. *And them what can't see me, I see you all the better,* says the troll. *Give me a lick of your face, says he. Cry, I loves my wicked salty.*

"Pretend all you want to be a big boy. Your face is red as a berry, but it's only so long you can bottle it all up. And then don't blame me when you start bawling. You can't say I didn't tell you so. And crying will only bring him out to you all the faster. First he ate all that pretty woodwork on the bed, all the way up to its roof and all the way down to the floor. He crunched through the bed's pretty walls and doors as if they were *krumkakes*. Then the feather mattress and pillows and quilt, from the cloth skin to the stuffing, licking every feather as he shoved it into his big, stinking mouth filled with big brown teeth with gaps between them that make him awfully angry and frustrated, as stuff always gets caught between them and he has to pick away at it with a toothfork he made from a hay rake. That's why trolls slobber so much. It's their butter and their sauce, and it helps the dry stuff down.

"Not that you're dry. You're juicy as a peach. You still don't see the troll? If you were good, you'd see him, for *There. He. Is. He is the bed.* Yes, that's the troll right there. *The bed.* He only has to eat something to pretend to be it. And tonight when we get into bed, just think. You'll be sleeping in the lap of him, or in his—"

"Enough!" yelled Pastor Kvak.

Afterwards, he was both ashamed he'd listened as long as he had, and glad. His son never slept in bed again, but curled up in corners like the vagrants and the dispossessed—dressed ready to run.

That was only one of many reasons that added up (unwittingly supplied by his parishioners) that Ommund was now nursemaid and mother to the child whose mother died from childbirth.

After they came home from Kjell's first deathbed, Ommund said "I was very proud of you, how you were not afraid. You see, it was silly to be afraid of that nice old lady."

Kjell took his thumb out of his mouth (a habit his father had hoped the *brunost* sticks would put an end to). "What a big snore she had."

"And what more did you see? Didn't you see something beautiful coming out of her mouth and nose and... sort of like me with a pipe, but prettier see-through colors."

His son eyes suddenly clamped shut and plump red lips puckered in the effort not to cry.

"Don't be afraid. I'm *glad* you saw it, son. For now, let it be our secret. When you're old enough, I'll explain."

Only ten years later did Kjell tell his father that he'd seen none of that. He'd screwed his eyes tight against seeing *him what will not be denied,* the salivating troll. The old lady's bed, all decorated and cozy, was all too familiar. All he had to do was open his eyes or move, and the troll would know.

They'd never discussed that plotting nursemaid who so obviously wanted a bed to herself, and a child too terrified to disturb her with so much as a peep. Pastor Kvak had never seen his son cry. And besides, Kjell was the product of biology, not some miracle from God or a bundle dropped down the chimney. Son must take after father, so son would be born too rational to believe in trolls, Thor, or anysuch *dritt*.

Blindast er den som ikkje vil sjå.

"I insist, Kjell. You must become an artist."

The pastor's face was wreathed with clouds, so forcefully had he pulled on his pipe.

"I was weak when I was young. In those days, going to church was still compulsory. What other living could one have that assured you that no matter how useless you were, you'd never starve? And what other living gives you as much free time to pursue your interests?"

"So you want me to become an artist. Not a scientist?"

"Not any old artist."

"Any old starving artist, you mean."

"Let science be your guide. But you can't live off it."

"Then why did you lead me down the science path?"

"To open your eyes, son. To use your senses. If you'd seen without just reading the words, you'd remember what Humboldt admitted. *The present state of science appears as a blank.* If only he could have been an artist, he would have changed the world. Why else did he write—here, must I read it for you? I see I must. *Man learns to know the external world through the organs of the senses. Phenomena of light proclaim the existence of matter in remotest space, and the eye is thus made the medium through which we may contemplate the universe.*"

"So you want me to compete with all the new photography to paint the stars."

"Blindest is he who doesn't wish to see! Since you could hold a pencil, you've drawn the phenomena of death. Yet in not one of your pictures do you show the phenomenon itself. The... the... I cannot fill your head with my theories. And no one else has put forward any observation, let alone an explanation. I have not the talent to show, and am but a simple pastor. You have extraordinary ability, such wasted talent."

Kjell's throat stuck.

"You are a blank who's studied science," said Pastor Kvak. "It's your *senses* that need to learn."

Kjell had worried about his father's senses for—well, forever. The day after that first visit to a deathbed, his father gave him his first block of paper, a pencil, and a scrap of *lefse.* He told the boy to draw some lines, and then showed him how to rub them out with the pliable potato flatbread. Not even twenty-four hours later, little Kjell was propped up on a family bible on the highest chair in a crowded apartment. His father just pointed and said, "Draw what you see."

He drew as well as he was capable. This time he was ready for the rattle, the open mouth he wanted to run away from. The drawing was hardly more than unrecognizable scribbles.

By Kjell's fifth birthday and forty-ninth death, Pastor Ommund Kvak knew his son was Mozart of the pencil. Kjell's pictures were full of intricate detail and standardization. He had nothing to compare them to, nor was he trained. He just drew.

If they'd talked, Kjell might have told his father what he'd learned: *Every deathbed, just as every person, is unique and yet so familiar, it's hard not to think the body hasn't lived and died a million times before.*

At the age of ten, Kjell knew his father was lying when the pastor announced to the congregation that he was taking a sabbatical for a month to get closer to God, and that he was taking his son to undergo a spiritual experience fit for the son of a pastor.

They took their first trip abroad to a place called Jenna. Ommund had ploughed the way with a long private correspondence.

Ernst Haeckel had built up a reputation for being a human cactus. Known as a graceless curmudgeon, he couldn't have been kinder to the boy. Nor more generous.

He never offered food or drink to boy or father. There was too much else to share, to teach, to reveal or marvel as the unknown of.

What Ommund wished Kjell to learn in particular, was the magic that was really just observation followed by experiment and increasingly refined technique. Ommund zeroed in on Haeckel's obsession, so all were not at peace. There was no resting. Only hard work, experiment, and thrill.

For Ernst Haeckel had taught himself how to paint the almost unseen, in all its detail and quite unearthly hues. Haeckel's life's work was built on his studies and subsequent watercolors of jellyfish and their even more see-through neighbors in the sea, the Siphophorae.

Ommund had previously sketched much glasswork, as the bed table of the dying always holds their last glass.

But these living creatures were far more subtle.

As Kjell practiced, Haeckel threw him a comment now and then, and the two men went back to discussing many things.

Soon enough, they were back in Oslo, and life went on as before, Kjell accompanying his father and sketching the scenes. The parishioners were so used to the two that no one thought it strange. "You see it now. Surely you do," the pastor always said to his son. The people watching always smiled. They approved strong disapproving taskmasters. It spoils the young to praise them. And who knows what the boy could leave out. We wouldn't want that! For the story went that by capturing those last moments on paper, the son was helping the father to capture all the ugliness of life, like a mousetrap does a mouse. This allowed the faulty person easier entry up there.

Of course, life for Kjell wasn't all painting and death-beds. With help from Haeckel, Pastor Kvak built up a library of such scientific formidability, his parishioners would have burnt it to a pile of ashes if they'd known. Kjell was a most eager student, always badgering his willing father for more. They made the nursery into a lab, too, full of spirit lamps and wonderfully evil-smelling stuffs.

Science, the bright sun of the age, burnt brightly behind the curtains.

But as the nursemaids warned, it's foolish for a child to think anyone can be safe in bed.

One dawn after a particularly long death, Pastor Kvak and his son arrived home. "Show me," said Ommund.

Kjell handed him a sheaf of pages. His father looked over the first, the second, the third—all the way to the twelfth and last, and dropped them on the floor.

"It's time you grew up, boy," said Pastor Kvak. "Fifteen years already, and you're still as observant as a potato."

That's when he told Kjell he had to become an artist. Only then might the boy learn to see.

He sent him to the best schools in places the pastor had never been. London, Paris, Vienna, Berlin. There was no arguing with the old man.

Kjell was lucky, in a way, that he got to see his father on

his deathbed. It was only the two of them, and thus, it saved Kjell the embarrassment of anyone hearing what his father had always hoped he'd see—all the souls pouring out of the heads, ears, mouths, of the lucky few. "The colors," he said, his last words.

> *Alle vil vere herre, ingen vil bere sekken.*
> Everyone wants to be a gentleman;
> nobody wants to carry the sack.

"Nature is not only all that is visible to the eye. Hey girl, two more here," Edvard Munch says to Kjell Kvak. "Nature also includes the inner pictures of the soul."

They'd met in this cozy little dive on the Bjørvika waterfront for a tot or two of *akevitt* as breakfast, which had stretched to a few appetite whetters for lunch hours ago.

Kvak laughs, his eyes merry but the sound has a ragged edge. "You're such a fool."

Munch is famous and rich, but skills? Kvak spits on the floor. Munch doesn't even paint decent size works. *And I can't get anyone to come to my place.* (Kvak's been making like an iceman for fourteen years now, schlepping his painting on his back.) *And no one has EVER noticed Adam*, shrunken little Adam, looking up towards Eve like a mouse looks up Galdhøpiggen Mountain.

He hates that Munch has become famous from painting something the man either doesn't understand or has seriously lied about. The man is a coward, a humbug, a fraud.

They've never talked about it, but it amazes Kvak that the scene hasn't turned into a tourist trap like Venice's Bridge of Sighs. For every evening of the short but precious summer, the light on that bridge shows souls flying from people's mouths and ears and eyes, thick as pigeons in St. Marks Square. And in the winter—in the winter, that is when you cannot see but you can hear—above the last rattle of a freezing drunk, a hand-muffled cough of a starving widow, below the slicing oars of wind—the slither, slip, pop out of the—the souls—all those alot of souls of a person.

Kvak doesn't know what to think about the souls flying out. He had never understood how his father could stomach any philosophy. But if only they'd talked. Had Pastor Kvak actually got out and *seen*, why would he wish that on anyone, let alone his own son. He couldn't have, or it would have chilled his bones, made him afraid of life itself. Souls forcing their way out of the living—*who keep on living.*

It can happen to anyone. And it means that you can never feel you're talking to a live man. You can never feel you're fucking a live woman.

Since Kvak was driven to record it for his own sanity, he's seen cats—and learned for a fact—that the cat's meow in the darkest night is many syllabled from the shoving clots of souls flying out. "Which goes to prove," Kvak says, "They bask and prowl in heaven, singe in hell. And we're the only ones supposed to."

Munch must have spied upon me while I painted the *Flight of Each Man's Souls,* before I painted over it. Then the bastard copied me, but lowered the style to his level—pure Munch! Shallow and flashy at the same time. "Flattered, I'm sure," mumbles Kvak who talks to himself so much, he never hears it.

Munch must have followed me and hasn't known to see. That sometimes made more sense to Kvak, as Munch was not only short on creativity and imagination, but found no shame in going to Paris to say he drinks with all the most revolutionary artists—the successful ones. *Munch is so bourgeois—so afraid of being judged a lunatic, clapped into Gaustad sykehus.*

Not that Kvak could think *Gaustad sykehus* without shuddering. His father had begged him to quit his commercial art so that he could "See. Go and see!"

Begged and begged. But the old man was so obsessed, not only forgot to eat. He forgot that the world is too damn carnal to live on seeing alone. It was only when Kvak went to visit him one day that he learned that the retired pastor was now a resident in *Gaustad sykehus*. Kjell never learned to his satisfaction whether his father had gone voluntarily or been consigned by the old ladies that infested his building.

Kjell rushed there, cursing the horse-clogged streets. The asylum was large as a palace, but warm. He found his father, not in bed, but in a room with tall aspidistras along the walls and climbing tomatoes in the internal windowboxes. A person could mistake it for a conservatory, except for the bars on the windows. A doctor and an orderly were talking with him, not just of him, till they noticed Kjell, and immediately bristled, ready to throw him out. They were quite welcoming and rather fascinated when his father rushed to shake his hand.

"You must have much to talk about," said the doctor. "But please see me before you leave."

"I'll make sure of that," said the orderly.

Kjell left the place with his fears and guilt somewhat lessened. All the women who'd always buzzed around his father would be horrified. Pastor Kvak was being taken care of with a mixture of scientific curiosity, respect, and no-nonsense "Eat." No one referred to him as a pastor. Indeed, there might as well have been a ban placed on the word God being uttered, the place was so enlightened. "We are glad that he recognized you," said the doctor. "And he didn't look aggravated, but it's best you give him time to adjust. He needs to be sufficiently flooded with the visual and oral stimulations we are building up for him. Only then can his delusions be shed. But don't you worry about his visions. We see this so much in those susceptible to belief."

Kjell agreed to give his father time to adjust. He didn't tell the doctor that they had formed a pattern years ago. He would see his father, who would badger him about seeing until he almost lost his temper. Then he wouldn't see his father for months. Always it had been the same. "You must think of nothing but art. Don't burn your eyes with all those shoes and bicycles and pretty girls. How it breaks my heart that you use your gifts just to make enough money to live. You must become an artist. Only then will you finally, *see!*"

He didn't think his father ever missed him as such. But this visit had been different. For the first time in twenty-six, no, twenty-seven years, the words *art, artist, see,* didn't pass through his father's lips. Ommund chattered brightly about the tomatoes in the windowboxes. Kjell hadn't known before, that his father could act.

Kjell quit work the next morning and took the long trip back to the *sykehus,* dreading the joy on his father's face at the news that Kjell, at last, was going to do his bidding.

"My trunk," his father said, "Take my striped trousers."

Lykken og ulykken bor vegg i vegg.
Happiness and accident live next door.

Everyone was hailing revolutionary art—so much so that artists were meeting and talking and flashing kroner like a gaggle of old biddies at cards.

He would have moved to an attic but his needs were too great, so instead, he cajoled from the chief a high inside wall area at the Grønlandsleiret Fire Station, where suddenly none of the men on duty were tempted to sneak out for their just-one-glass of poison.

Almost two months later, Kjell interrupted his work to visit his father again. The fire station chief had asked him to spend the day away because they needed the whole space for some exercises. Kjell was happy at the enforced break. He'd been working hard, but it was harder than he'd thought it could be, to work with no direction. He'd mocked up something that he'd thought might do as an impressive *oeuvre,* but honestly, every day he thought more frequently *what's the point?* He missed the vacuous pleasure and security of painting to deadlines—be it a glittering pickled herring, a bottle of crystal-clear *akevitt,* or a heavily booked young woman whose look would be passé by next season.

Ommund was not to be found. Kjell roamed the halls back and forth, till finally, he recognized the orderly who immediately took him by the arm, walking brisky. "We didn't know how to contact you," said the orderly, which was true. Would *you* have been willing to tell an insane asylum, "I live at Grønlandsleiret Fire Station where I sleep on the floor."

His father was in bed, the only time Kjell had ever seen him in bed.

"Doctor Griesel, get my son paper and pencil. My son, the artist." He turned to Kjell with a smile. "The colors."

Paper and pencil came too late, but it would have been obscene to draw. *This was all there is to see, really. Only the thousandth death, as different and alike as all the others.*

Kjell left the asylum with the rest of the long day on his hands. For the first time, he spent it walking, looking. His chest hurt. He could feel his heart sobbing—sharp, sucking, dry heaves.

He walked beside the bright waters, he picked through stinking alleys. He prowled the docklands like the cat seeking rats who've stuffed themselves with fish.

He got two rattles without having to see them: the choked geyser of vomit of a flat-on-his-back drunk. The man must have been hidden behind a pile of garbage. Kjell couldn't find him. And coming up from a vent in a fetid basement, the common last rattle of a young woman, followed by a man cursing every god modern and old.

Kjell tried for the first time in his life to stop listening, to stop looking at what he could see. He tried to loosen his focus, throw his rational mind to the wolves.

Nothing. That night, he curled in an alley for a few hours, and then took off again. Many hours later on that summer night that looked more like day, with nothing in his stomach and a hole in his sole, he saw.

Beautiful? If hell is beautiful.

He had to put it to canvas. He was frantic to.

All his innate talent and learned skills drove his mind and hands. The picture would have put Haekel to shame. Kvak didn't pretty anything up, didn't fudge an iota to fit anyone's aesthetic. The picture was not just a painting. It was an illustration. The only way he could drive it from his mind and keep it out was to stick every scintilla of the scene onto the canvas, not just every detail anatomically, but emotionally. Get it all down. And then cover it all up. Only after it was sufficiently painted over could he think again, not want to hide in a corner of the fire station.

He'd never expected to *see*, but having seen...

Ommund Kvak wasn't a father to get close to, so Kjell didn't feel bad that the old man had died thinking his son a disappointment for not having ever seen. If they'd talked about it as the *sykehus* and been overheard, he'd never have been let out.

Still, the old man had freed Kjell to become the great artist he had hidden from the world till now.

He hadn't known what to paint before, but it came to him out of nowhere. Now he really threw himself into painting his masterpiece, taking revolution at its word.

Watching him was the healthy diversion the firemen needed—and he was a most theatrical artiste, moving his arms like some conductor, cursing richly, sighing indecently—creating, to the men's confused, ignorant delight—a nude of their own—surely nothing their wives and mothers would ever know about. Sure, she was dangerous. Aren't they all? The rest of the stuff in the painting—well, artists are artistes, are they not. The men ignored all the rubbish to focus on *the beauty over our bar*, as the chief was wont to say with a wink.

But as everybody knows, good luck is loaned, not owned. One midshift when all the men were in the station, many watching the artist paint, he stood back suddenly and visibly held his breath till the pipe smokers in the room marvelled.

He exhaled, grabbed a virgin brush, dipped it and made the last operatic strokes. Very minimal, very stylish. Utterly illegible, except for the date. Two of the men clapped, one man took off his cap and held it to his chest, and the others looked at each other in confusion, feeling like they'd arrived at St. Peter's Gate without washing the smoke of fire off their bodies. One was so relieved it was finished, his eyes misted.

The only thing left for the painting was for the paint to dry. The men didn't know about paint drying. Something had ended, and none of the men felt prepared. Surely, it was easier to throw oneself—with confidence—into a burning tenement. All but one of them privately thought it would be grand to treat the painter to the Olympen for a real singup and tankard-clanking time, but the sobriety that had infected the station resulted in them asking him to stay for a little coffee party with cake one of the men was sent to the bakery to buy.

Only God or the Devil knows how many men privately thought the woman on the painting disgusting, and in what ways. But for now, in concert, the applause was deafening, demanding an encore at least.

The chief begged the artist to start another, to no avail. First, Kvak had taken the times at their reputation, had studied the booming successes of the revolutionary greats. In all the capitals that count, these men were being rewarded with not just reputation but riches. And it was plain as the noses on their faces, most of these other successful artists were studied frauds, often copying each other, not a genuine expression amongst them, and precious little skill. If any of the others had tried to make their living painting chocolate wrappers, they would have starved. But the revolution provided for these *poseurs*, so it should heap upon Kvak.

And he was skint. Sure, he'd paid nothing for his fire station studio. But he was getting dizzy spells from hunger. The firemen had assumed it was the artist's frenzied passion forcing him never to leave his love. They once in a while offered him a sausage or a cup of tea when he looked a bit too weakened by artful lust, little did they know.

But now that he'd dismantled his scaffolding, he seemed suddenly to realize their presence, and to be embarrassed.

The chief asked him out for a breath of air. They walked like men late for an appointment, leaving clouds of breaths like two racing steam trains. The fire chief set the pace, his intensity quickening his steps. "Is there any way we can persuade you, sir, to continue to grace our station?"

Kvak hmmed and mmmed and pulled at his beard—not at all like the so coarse, they were straightforward men the chief had under him. The chief had to be patient—to draw the artist out.

Finally, the chief and Kvak both needed a little warmup tipple before going back to the station to announce that Mr. Kvak had consented to let the firemen convert a part of the stables in their yard to become his salon for showing clients. And for his studio, he would continue to let the station be his domain.

One fireman was silent when the rest of them cheered. As he'd observed, others loved the painting and the artist, as innocents love evil when it's dressed to kill. So as soon as he'd been aware that the artist had signed and dated the thing that he tried to avoid eye contact with, his thoughts were naturally, it's late today but tomorrow this, this "man" named Kjell Kvak will sell the abomination and get himself a studio so big and fancy, he's far away from here.

He'd never said anything but he'd seen a side of the artist no one else had—less than a week after the artist had been installed.

The fireman had been tempted to have a drink or few on the way to work that day, having, the shift before, half fallen through a collapsing wooden staircase while carrying a woman over one arm and her toddler over the other. So he wasn't late to his shift, but he knew he needed to busy himself in some maintenance job, alone. The chief had said he would be visiting his ailing mother. Benterod, for that was the tempted one's name, heard the chief's booming voice just as he entered the door. In panic, he ducked behind a row of spare suits hanging on the wall. A moment later, four bells rang, emptying out the station of everyone but him, and the oblivious artist at work in front of him.

Benterod was thinking of climbing out when the artist did a strange thing, even for an artist. He took two broad brushes, dipped them and slapped them all over the canvas as quickly as an illicit poster paster slaps glue on a prominent wall, but this wasn't glue. It was paint, the color of flesh. He painted over his charcoal sketch, removing all the human bushes and one lascivious leg.

Once the canvas was totally covered in flesh pink, he took up different brushes, and in a frenzied dance that would do St. Vitus proud, he painted a scene that, frankly, made Benterod stuff a fist in his mouth to keep his teeth from chattering. Benterod decided during the three hours that it took for Kvak to paint that scene on the bridge, and the five minutes to cover it up, that Kvak could be nothing less than the Devil himself. No one could paint so fast, could show a scene on mere canvas that was a vision of a hell so strange and real, you could smell the brimstone in the poor man's brain. And then nobody but the very Devil himself would, with a flick and flack, cover it up again in more flesh-colored undercoat, to innocently start his previous painting anew.

Asbjørn Benterod slunk out of the station unseen but a nose could have followed him with no problem. He didn't care. He had to run home to his mother.

Just that day at her weekly appointment, she'd been saying "He's too young to undertake such dangers, just thirteen though he's taller than you and shaved when he was ten. Oh, I feel so dirtied. No, please don't say anything. You're the only one I can tell. He said he'd run away to sea if I didn't let him. And you know those owners have no scruples. He said he'd support me even if I drove him to do it by sending money from Patagonia. So I had no choice. The fire station's just a block from us, so at least I can make sure he's fed right. But what mother gets her son false papers to prove he's old enough to… Oh, I should be taking care of him. But I'm a silly. Here, I thought you mightn't have got over your catarrh, and from your voice it's clear you're still not taking care of yourself, so I made you these pastilles."

The police doctor unfolded his hands to accept her package. This was the most she'd ever said about her life—a life he'd pieced together from little crumbs she'd dropped, and bits he'd cobbled from his own investigations.

His knuckles hurt, he'd clamped them together so hard. He'd not touched this woman for years. Truly, he had for years tried his hardest to lessen the indignity of her having to come to these appointments. Indeed, the most dangerous women were ones he never saw, the hidden, unmentioned killers. He would have liked to hang a public health notice on the Royal Palace: *Never Marry a Widow Known for her Virtue.*

"You had to do what you had to do," he said from the samovar where he made Russian tea with perhaps more rattling of cups than usual. As he put hers on the desk, his voice was low. "But I wish you had come to me about those papers. And I have an announcement to make."

"Herr Doktor," she said when he was finished, taking a wafer from the plate he offered. "I am shocked. You look too young to retire."

"I had hoped you would wish me the best of fishing and mushroom gathering."

"That need be unstated," she said crisply. She didn't smile but he did, marveling once again at how flexible society is, when allowed to be sensible. Here was your model citizen, Aagot Benterod, widow of a sea captain who had died mysteriously the night before his ship landed from its most successful whaling expedition. His widow only knew about it when the oldest man from his crew, someone who'd sailed with him for a dozen years, made a visit to her house and told her. "Aagot Benterod," he'd said, "If we ever catch that *Fanden*, the devil who sold the ship and your husband's pay, we'll freeze his balls, excuse me, and hang him from his eyes with blubber hooks."

The crew had been paid, of course, because they landed with the goods. And they never got the opportunity to right the wrong done to their captain, for the past owner lived in a different strata, high above mere seamen. And besides, a captain falling out of his ship, dead drunk as all the powers that be insisted, deserved pay as much as a wooden parrot deserves a cracker.

But what was she to do? She owned a large collection of scrimshaw, a little ship's bell hanging on an elaborately knotted rope. A respectable widow with a child of two, with only two available means of support: sewing, or providing that other service that was always needed and could be undertaken by women with weak eyes.

The police doctor and the prostitute/captain's widow were probably both quietly reminiscing while outside the door, the crowd blustered as usual—chaotic and incoherent.

Prostitution was strictly illegal, but sensibly policed. What the government wanted was women like Aagot Benterod, women of some class. *A respectable woman has no sex drive, will never lure men to their death. Men need women to service what single men can't get and married women mostly don't provide. And because women, even the best of them, are weak, we need to make sure they can't kill us with their diseases.* Thus, the world turns round though red tape might try to tie it up.

The police doctor rose and took their cups. "Let the winds blow, Moeder Benterod. Let's have another cup of tea."

He wanted to look at her longer, the better to screw up his courage. He half marveled at himself. She looked the same as the day almost twenty years ago when she'd first walked in. Her skin so fine and clear, it was colorless. Her hair, simply dressed, the white of oiled paper. Her eyes, two frozen pools. Of course she had colorless lips. Her slender build was muscular, not soft. And down *there*, she was not only hairless, but had no smell. Not like those women outside the door who had to be stopped, but who were no more stoppable than plagues in Bergen. Their lush dark bushes, so fetid, fatal yet irresistible. Their faces, irresistible fevers of color and shadow—nothing safe, yet the nothing tame of it was all the temptation most men need to be caught.

The police doctor had at first felt sorry for this woman, assuming she'd starve. By the end of her first year in the profession, he'd stopped examining her and begun the ritual of the tea. One of the reasons was, he wanted an excuse to watch her hands. She never made a false movement or expression, yet her fingers made him think of a rippling spring.

They'd talked of many things over the years, including their wishes to see the world beyond Oslo's horizon. They never spoke of her clients. He suspected that she specialized in seamen from the lively descriptions she gave of places she said she'd only read about. As they say, a blind hen may pick up a grain, but this woman had picked up a harvest.

He fiddled with his spoon. It must have been a few minutes since either had spoken. *So when I told her I'm retiring, why hadn't she asked me about the places I'll go?*

Herr Doctor," she said, "Duty calls."

She placed her cup and saucer on his desk. He noticed with a secret pleasure that her hand wasn't quite its sure fluid self.

"As I hope to call upon you," he said.

She nodded once before opening and closing the door by her own bare hand.

He left the door closed for one more long minute. The smell of her— snow-thaw over moss—would be smothered by the next client.

She took the trolley straight home, but as soon as she

opened the door, she smelled something wrong.

Asbjørn Benterod was sitting at the scrubbed table, his head in his hands. This was no time to ask questions.

She poured him a tumbler of cod liver oil and tipped it into his helpless mouth as if he were still five.

"Why do you think the writing is on the wall," she said before she filled the tin tub with hot water for his bath, and then served him a dinner many a magnate would have cried over, it made you feel so coddled. O, big little Asbjørn all grown up and such a child.

The framed writing on the wall was in a rather large and simple cross-stitch. As her son dried off, he wondered how it was that whenever you looked at it, it was already watching you. It seemed to follow you. *Beste middel mot å bli drukken er å halde seg edru*, it said. The best remedy against getting drunk is keeping sober.

As she tucked him into his bed nook, she said, "Never hide your drink. It always betrays you."

If you only knew, thought her son. He hated the taste of it. Hated the secrecy and waste of money. But *drink hides your fears.*

O, 1892! Its dependable vices, its steadfast revolutions.

From a 2012 advertorial:

The style is steroidally original—a vividly colored clash of Expressionist/Mannerist/Art Nouveau and pre-Postmodern tones. Long languorous strokes in the absinthe green of some-one who the sun never touches, highlight the curves of the First Woman's naked body, dipping down to a frenzy of short burnt-flesh-black Van Goghic slashes, the recesses of her navel, the trail of hair running down to her densely forested triangle, leading out and down each thigh, 'like a trail of army ants' (*Rolling Stone*). Eve's whole body seems to sweat, the synergy of strokes giving her unnatural life, 'as exposed as a new check-in at a morgue,' while at the same time, making her face pure Impression—all smudges and dashes, light and shadow. Yet that mouth, those eyes—unnerving—all the more so against the Rembrandtic realism and chiaroscuro in the depiction of each shrunken, half-eaten apple in the chaise lounge-shaped pile she is stretched out on, 'like an odalisque in an ossuary'.

Kvak might have liked that description. In 1892, the combination of styles, as if he couldn't decide or couldn't discard his technical skill—repelled dealers, salons, collectors, of course—anyone thinking to buy it, let alone hang it on their wall. One's reputation could be compromised, for that mishmash of styles proved one knows nothing about art, or isn't solidly in the right camp.

Early in the dawn of the 21st century noughties, Axa Røsland, founder/leader of the Oslo-based UGB (Urban Guerrilla Brigade) collected and delighted in quoting unknowingly incriminating brags by Oslo's Developer/Local Government Complex. "Nothing in Fjord City is being left to chance and circumstances. Every bicycle stand and the edge of each flagstone are part of the design. Surveillance cameras are already mounted." "The row of Bjorvika office buildings, befittingly baptized BARCODE, is a concept developed by… and Norwegian firms a-lab and Dark architects… It is already attracting prestigious tenants such as Pricewaterhouse Coopers."
The developers were up front when they stated, "BARCODE will create that signature skyline Oslo never had. Our 400,000 m2 will be mainly for commercial use, but 400-500 apartments and substantial retail areas will also be developed."
BARCODE would not only destroy Oslo's low skyline, but its dark peepholes between the towers that cut off Oslo's view of the harbor would certainly make Oslo's signature skyline a gap-toothed troll smile in Modern Brutalist: *We l com to O slo*

And the champagne apartments, as they were known, would be a stake in the heart of Norway's precious *janteloven.* Hello societal stratification!

Røsland blogged and blogged, but somehow stopping evil with irony hadn't worked. So Røsland and her fellow guerrillas had started breaking into sites at night, looking with increasing desperation for *something* to wield against the Complex.

One black night they were prowling an ex-machine shop when she found something upstairs in the office. Taking up one whole wall was a huge antique chalkboard that must have been from the 1950s or even earlier and was painted with columns for jobs. The board had been spray-painted over in incoherent loops. Someone had also bashed one edge off. Hanging down from that lower left-hand edge was a scrap of—Belle Epoque hooker's dress? The colors were so garish. She bent down, sniffed and sneezed. The smell was so bad, it was simply marvelous. She had hoped Death. Murder. Jack the Ripper Settled Down in Oslo. But this was more Mummy—part resinous, part literally fishy.

Muscles popping, she unhooked the massive chalkboard. Odd how it had been hung, as if it had been meant to be flipped so it faced the wall.

So she carefully dropped it face down on the floor. What faced her was a canvas tacked to the frame as if the chalkboard were only the stiffener for the painting on the cloth.

Røsland, MFA'd to be an art historian/curator/dealer didn't recognize the idiosyncratic style, a nauseating mix expertly carried out as if Van Gogh and Rembrandt had buddy-painted a sampler for a poison-apple company. Well worth covering, insanity glowed from the canvas, or ingrained cultural nastiness. But value? Of course not. The work of a frustrated insane forger, as all forgers are.

Yet Røsland was desperate for a find, and this was funky enough—*weird* enough—*obsessively* magnificently crafted in all its repulsiveness and unsellability. Obviously, the painter was insane and had no money so this had to be recycled canvas. And it's obviously not professionally mounted. So... *Gaustad sykehus!* This painting, dated 1892 but with a typically psychotic bit of graffiti as signature, *has to be therapy.*

Axa Røsland felt a warm glow of nostalgia and fear. To a number of artists, this old nuthouse had become home. The insane asylum would have been costly to run, so it must always have been short of the folding stuff. A canvas this large must have been worked on by many, which explains the ensemble effect—always a disaster. But there had to be more than meets the eye. Ground-shakingly more. It was too large a canvas to be anything but a sane and compassionate artist's work, made for some reason into a stripped bed for insane artists to cavort on. The coldly rational side of Røsland pointed out that being a great artist, and compassionate, and altruistic—they just don't mix. But there was some reason someone valued this enough to hide it *here*—a machine shop. A supposed machine shop. There had to be something underneath the patients' group effort. Spread out flat on the floor at her feet was the key to saving this whole district, perhaps the soul of Oslo itself.

She didn't bounce anything off her fellow guerrillas who anyway wouldn't have been interested or wouldn't understand. At the moment, they were all oohing over some metal missed when the machine shop's contents were sold for scrap. "See this homemade model train," Aksel had shouted.

The time: 0200. Plenty. Røsland carefully pried all the tacks loose from the canvas and rolled it up into a giant cigar. She had to walk carefully down the stairs and out the door so as not to step on a stray steel shaving. But no one heard or saw. She shoved the cigar in the back of the brigade's van, a vehicle with great cover. The keys were on the seat, all readied by Petter for any eventuality—some emergency getaway, the brigade all piling in. With a light touch, she gunned the engine and took off.

An accident screwed up highway access at Biskop

Gunnerus' Gate, yet she still made the 0800 ferry from Larvik, landing in Hertshals, Denmark at 1245. Then it was highways all the way. The van was a joy. She hadn't ever owned a car. Petter delivered for a local bakery that didn't need to know he commandeered their one vehicle every night in case the brigade actually found something. Otherwise everyone had to drive exposed on their bicycles. At 0705, while downing a cup of coffee, she panicked, remembering her bike. It was leaning against the building. But *Petter* rushed into her tired, excited brain. He'd pick it up. After all, he'd lost his wheels.

Speeding forward along the delightfully fast highways, she only stopped again for coffee, lotsa coffees, and the inevitable pees. She reached Antwerp just past midnight. Nils buzzed her up so fast, he must have been watching the street. She'd only texted him from the ferry: *ges hoo? coming ur place 2nt.wots ur add? xxuptherev.* He answered three minutes later though they hadn't seen each other since the conference in Turin. From the length of the garbage he'd thumbed in, he must have started answering within seconds. Finally, at the end, he'd put his address.

Nils was obsessed with the wonders of technology—the second-class obsession in his life. The first was her. He was only a cog in the system, but so trustworthy and admiring— always wishfully yearning but never expecting to sleep with the legend, Axa Røsland, "the only real revolutionary I know."

While Axa showered and then ate the feast Nils had laid out for her arrival, he went to the university with the big cigar, and worked his magic on it.

She was sleeping in his bed when he knocked on his bedroom door and entered with a tray for her of warm sugar-dusted *poffertjes*, cold butter, honey from his own hive on the roof, and hot chocolate.

He was too shy to have kissed her awake or touched her at all, so he said brightly, "Breakfast! And now, the news."

She rubbed her eyes and stretched, ruining his favorite

workshirt, for work. He would never wear or wash it again (for in true revolutionary spirit, she hadn't packed, but lived off the land).

While she ate, he gave her the news.

"I found something."

He handed her a necklace he'd made for her. A new jump drive on a red lanyard.

She plugged it into his laptop—faster than her digging hers out of her bag.

He'd loaded the image he'd made and three crops of it. She looked at all four images briefly, hung the lanyard round her neck, and fingering the drive while she thanked him for his work. "That's alright," she assured him. "You did find *something*. It wasn't your fault it's worthless to the cause."

He had had a rather thrilling night. Always exciting to uncover something private, or unseen for millennia. And she seemed not *too* disappointed in him, as such. So he bottled his hurt in hope when she said, "Sure, it wasn't a bad idea, theoretically, to do more detailed analyses, but it was stupid to leave it there. Sorry, but I can't trust the institution and I gotta run, my love. We'll just have to pick it up, won't we."

A half hour went by in a blur. He'd not asked about the baker's van. Of course she must have stolen it to protect her activities as head of the UGB. She had such a full life, full of hidden layers.

But there was a high point at the end, after he'd made like a cat burglar in his own lab, and the rolled up painting was now safe in the baker's van. She actually kissed her jump drive and then him on the cheek. "Better scrub your night here," she said in that husky whisper of hers. "All your files. I couldn't have you losing your job, or worse, on my conscience."

"You don't have to tell me," he said. "Dokumenter glemmer ikke."

"Up the rev," he whispered to himself as he watched her drive away. Above him, leaning out from the venerable building, three gargoyles stared down, and an unknown number of cameras in their shadows.

Someone in the shadows *tch*ed to himself. The grizzled watchman, one month short of his pension, had witnessed their farewell. *I'll never understand people. That poor professor. What a fool he's making of himself, so in love with that girl, and she doesn't give a fig for him. But it serves him right, wanting an unskilled laborer. The smarties should leave the uneducated for us.*

As she drove, she had to be extra careful in the traffic. She wanted to *scream*. Nils had found so much more than Axa Røsland had imagined in her wildest, most post-revolutionary dreams.

Nils was an unsung master of judged technique—but Nils knew too much, including seeing her vomit in a trash bin before giving her paper in Bruges.

Besides, Nils was so very right. She had a lot of work to do.

Funny how parents can be utterly useless until they grow up. Axa's father, Øystein Løvold Røsland, was a very successful art dealer. As with all successful art dealers, his connections were his all—as closely guarded as the paintings in the Munch Museum *should* be.

And always, they had people or a person in to eat. Likely as not, Øystein would both prepare and serve it. Axa's mother might or might not be in, she always being wrapped up in her human rights lawyer life.

"Pappa," Axa said one Saturday afternoon when there was one guest, a museum curator. Axa had learned from experience that they came in ones. "So someone who doesn't know so much or who's too dumb to know anything finds you. And you sell the painting to some museum. And it's another find of the century."

"Sorry," said the curator, stifling a laugh. "Please go on."

"So you say it's some Pescaro or Oshofantastico Monkeybrain and everyone goes yay. Lemme have it. Then why didn't my teacher believe me when I said I didn't go to school last Thursday cuz I was sick?"

The curator's eyes were busy supervising his hands cutting into a tender slice of *pinnekøtt*.

"Axa," said her father. "Your teacher was right. Roger, I've got you a whole *pinnekøtt* to take home because you like it so. But I don't know if your Customs people will approve"

"They had better, Oyster. The closest we get to this in New York is pastrami. Americans don't understand lamb. And this ain't no pastrami."

He'd not had much to eat yet but had already indulged himself on Øystein's seductive *punsch*. It made him feel like skating dangerously, particularly because he'd suspected for some time, that one of the three sensations he'd bought from Øystein for the Met was, well, screw profanity. It never hurt anyone, not like the worst word in the English language, also four letters starting with F. But now that he'd argued for the f... and bought it (at that record-breaking price), he would have to stake his life on it or lose everything.

"Young lady," he said. "It's terrible that your teacher didn't believe you. We've got a saying you might take note of. It was uttered by one of our great sages. It ain't over till it's over."

The art dealer's eyes were cold as frozen berries when he turned to the curator with a smile. "And we've a saying. *Dokumenter glemmer ikke.* Never forget it, Axa. Roger, it's been fun."

Documents don't forget.

Without scratching the surface, the underpainting exposed by scanning macro x-ray fluorescence spectroscopy has become the center of their world for an unknown number of movements. But is what you know merely what you believe? What is "known" about this underpainting has been reported, speculated upon, feared, legislated upon, wished for; and spurred industries such as Perpetual Perma-plug, to stop.

Axa Røsland became such a minor celebrity, she was formally excommunicated from the UGB, though not by unanimous consent. Petter lost his job delivering for the bakery but Axa's spontaneous act and all the dedication she had put into saving the neighborhood, let alone the building, and all that self-sacrificial driving all the way to Paris with no break for herself—he'd been in love with her before—but he was hopelessly done for now. The other guerrillas also saw her as the moon while they were slugs, which only made them want to look up at her to swear.

Her interviewers always asked about that painting, *the secret painting*, how amazing she was to have suspected anything of worth under such a morbid, obscene of course, misogynistic, ugly scene dubbed by Rolling Stone: *Porn Eden*—the painting they couldn't help showing because it was by far the most interesting of the two. The other was frankly, too much like aboriginal art—visitors from space—weird shit coming out of some guy's head—crazy but not obscene.

As you know, pretty much overnight hundreds of millions of people were risable—many of them viewers and commentators who never saw *Porn Eden*. But you'd have to avert your eyes not to see. Eve's overtly sexual bits were blurred out on all US public networks till she looked like a projectile of vomit streaked over a *Peaceable Kingdom*. Tiny little shrunken Adam was blurred, too, till he looked like a blurt of the lion's crap.

Axa's nose twitched delightfully when she was animated, and she was as animated as a lit firecracker. She was a natural storyteller too. Her sleuthing to track down the artist—legend. For someone so young to make the find of the century—"incredible and amazing." You've got to see her telling it, so this isn't a patch on her, but: in 1349, a trading ship from pestilential England carrying lots of wool, seamen who'd died *en route* from the plague, and rats, ran aground as a ghost ship can, in Askøy, Norway. Rats and plague disembarked and scurried up the coast to Norway's biggest smoke, Bjørgvin (modern Bergen), wiping out just enough people to be a disaster but not enough to put out the plague. "Bergen suffers plagues so regularly you could set a generational clock by it."

And so family records are a complete mess, but there are ways to find if one is dedicated. Ole Hufthammer came from a little village a week north of Bergen. His grandfather was known as a seer. Seeing things no one else in the village could. Little Ole saw his first vision when he was five—a man with white smoke coming from his ears, nose, mouth. In the one surviving page from what is obviously a journal, he referred to that first vision, and how the character Santa Claus must have been invented by someone who either had or was witness to this *syndrom*. Ole was sent away by his father to escape another bout of plague which ultimately killed everyone in the Huftkhammer family, on both sides. This might however, be speculation.

What is known is that he traveled the world but was a hermit. Artists came privately to him for special tutorials, though this cannot be proven. It is only referred to in that one surviving page. What is known, however, is that the painting that he covered up is nothing less than the precursor to the painting that made Munch's reputation, and that he therefore painted over and over again, *The Scream*.

The hermit Hufthammer's unnamed *Pre-Scream* calls into question, to say the least, both Munch's story that the painting is about some mere scream, and the originality of Munch's vision, which looks like an apprentice's poor knockoff next to this masterwork of a moment.

As to the signed painting which the artist must be referring to when he says, "I must keep The Original Impregnation safe," we must assume he had his reasons. Axa Røsland has made it her life's work to find the trove, if there is any, of the hermit Hufthammer's *oeuvres*. So far, this is all there is—one extraordinary painting of greatly controversial tone and topic, the hidden work that has spawned speculation world-wide, and a popular-science name as well as warring global movements for the phenomenon seen throughout history by possibly more than the rare few, for as today, those who speak up should expect to be ridiculed. So quite naturally, it should be no surprise that Ole Hufthammer was almost impossible to find and verify as the artist. As Axa Røsland says, only through sources can one ever be sure. Documents don't lie. She still has not been able to track his life down to its end.

Naturally, in all the interest in the painting behind the painting—meaning and speculated meaning—the mystery of an artist trying to leave a message, and then covering it up—and the almost loss to humanity of this mystery for the Ages—there wasn't enough time to talk about the evils of redevelopment.

Alder fører sikkert til det som er verre.
Age probably leads to something worse.

One day not long ago, a man in a nursing home in Helgesensgate Street, Oslo, was thinking of past times when on the unavoidable, perpetually on TV, an attractive young woman's twittering was cut to a slow panning view of a painting. That horrible, woman-hating painting. And then, horror of horrors, a sort of bleached out view, like a war picture of WWI, of the terrifying painting underneath. Like an x-ray, or a body dug from a soggy trench.

He fumbled for his hearing aids, and got one in. "As the only surviving work of this unique genius," the young woman was saying, "it would be impossible, not to mention crude and materialistic, to put a price on a painting you, ah, like to call so naughtily Porn Eden, or the painting underneath, which is so scientifically, not to mention religiously impor-tant, I haven't the training to talk about it. But its auction will help fund more of my research into its immortal but mysterious artist, Ole Hufthammer."

"Dra til helvete," the old man shouted. "Faen ta deg!"

A nurse rushed up, though he hadn't called. "Asbjørn Benterod," she said. "I'm surprised at you."

Her eyes were twinkling. Always good to see a bit of life and spunk in the old ones. There's no substitute for life. And he was her favorite. Always so interested in others, clean in his person and caring of the staff to a fault. She'd had to tell him that he shouldn't try to hold in what nature wants to let out.

But he wasn't smiling now. Something had so deeply disturbed him that he'd sworn.

"Let's go into the garden," she said, wheeling him away from all the interested eyes.

You had to be patient with him. He hadn't a lot of breath, and this had taken a lot out of him. "... and so, she's lying, I tell you. That's the picture. The painting underneath has the wrong colors in their picture. It was so alive."

His transparent hand gripped his lap blanket. "Alive as a day-old dead man in a trench. She knows nothing. The artist she talks about. I'd know his name better than I can spell my own. He always wore striped trousers. I bet she doesn't know that. He used the nail on his left little finger to paint. His name was Kjell Kvak. And I can show you where he painted them. That terrifying horrible thing he hid. He couldn't be human. Oh, she doesn't know the first of it. The speed he painted that abomination underneath. Like painting the Mona Lisa in the time it takes to eat a herring. You believe me, mother, don't you?"

"Of course I do," said the nurse.

"Shouldn't I tell everyone the truth?"

"The truth," she said. "If you do, then we'd have to let them know how old you'll be next Tuesday. And everyone will come around and bother you. But wouldn't it be fun having a birthday party for you on television?"

She was crouched in front of him, so it was easy to take a tissue from her pocket to wipe a tear away. "Let's not worry about the silly world," she said. "I hate television as much as you do, so why don't you and I just have a private little party next Tuesday."

She was glad as she wheeled him back, that he couldn't see her face. Just when you think you've seen too much to feel, you stab yourself in the eyes again, being cruel to be kind.

The old man seemed to calm down remarkably fast, but his hand shook more than normal when he used his spoon at lunch.

He cursed himself for his outburst. He hadn't wanted his mother to tell anyone that it would be his hundredth birthday. First, she'd got him papers that said he was eighteen. Then later, his stepfather had got him papers that said he was eighteen, and then later, he'd got his own papers—so many times, he'd lost track. It didn't matter that every time, he'd needed them so he could help people. Fireman, marine rescuer, avalanche digger, resistance fighter, lighthouse keeper, medical orderly at Bergen's leper hospital, security guard. That was no excuse. His mother felt dirtied the first time. It didn't matter that his stepfather, the police doctor, said you must make your own truth. He was long dead. *But she is here and I must protect her. If I get found out, she'll not survive the shame.*

The nurse found him unusually quiet the next morning. "It's only to be expected," she said brightly. "Let's not watch any stupid television."

"And let's not talk of birthdays?"

"If you prefer." She had the seniority to stop any celebration, so his hundredth birthday passed as days do with the very old in care.

He was so relieved when he went to sleep on Tuesday night that he relaxed more than usual. He'd always hated lies, but they had seemed so necessary when he was younger. If only anyone knew how much a lie his birthday was, he'd be all over the TV, in prisoner's clothes.

Ever since seeing the Devil at work, he'd had a dread of meeting him after death. So he hadn't wanted to die. It got easier after he stopped work, and now it had become a habit, keeping alive. He was so old now, he wasn't sure if he could die.

Yet another reason not to let anyone know. His mother would be so shamed to have mothered a cowardly freak.

He put a smile on his face. She was coming to wheel him into lunch.

The man of many names and dates might well be the oldest man in the world, but then there are the others.

Edvard Munch missed seeing Kjell Kvak get up off the stones slickened by pee, vomit, fish parts, and all the filth tramped in on the bottom of men's soles. Not that it would have mattered to Kvak. He walked away from the waterfront towards town. Something niggled at him for a few blocks, and then evaporated, to his relief. Soon he saw that a lone woman and he would cross paths. She looked quite as carefree. "Beautiful night," he said. "A peach," said she.

That was going to be all the known unknowns, but Breaking News from The Mirror:

Celebrity Fights with Geek over Lost Treasure

"Utter s….," tweeted Axa Røsland in the politest of tirades against what many call "the find of the century". Her charming twitching nose must be painfully out of joint, all due to reports that an expert at a Dutch university has found the lost journals of the world's most mysterious artist, Ole Hufthammer…

We caught up with her in Sydney, on the set of I'm a Celebrity … Get Me Out of Here! where she calmed down long enough to say, "Who does this guy think he is. This is nothing short of a preposterous example of fake news generated to support an armchair explorer of the geekiest kind." Nils Boorland, the expert who found and analyzed the treasure trove, plays every day with multimillion dollar equipment we can't pretend to understand, and is a renowned expert at finding stuff the rest of us cannot see...

CODE
OF THE
NEW FOURTH

INGER. Rose. Bet you thought we couldn't play. Meet Nathan, my toy boy."

"Boy toy," said Rose.

Estelle refrained from pursing her lips (wrinkles!) and smiled. She'd sashayed in on Nathan's strong arm. Their companions were still devices that kept them permanently humbled. Rose had a walker at her elbow. Ginger, the two-speed chair she practically lived in.

Rose's mouth formed the shape of a squeezed lemon slice. "Your so-called Nathan must feel lucky."

"Luck has nothing to do with it," said Estelle's escort.

"What cheek!" spattered Rose.

"So sue me."

Ginger brayed hoarsely. "This Nathan of yours has your Morris' sense of humor."

"I'd like to think it's my own, Mrs. Silvers."

"So would Morris have." Pow-bam! Rose was in form, though she'd not have guessed possible, a robot with an ego.

Nathan seated Estelle, and owl-like, swiveled to regard Rose. "Mrs. Katz, pray keep your disparagements to yourself."

Ginger's eyes sparkled. "Where did you get it, er, him?" She sounded and looked like Marilyn Monroe, should she have lived so long. Her voice was husky with emphysema. She'd never treated herself to jealousy, but couldn't help wishing she could afford this vision of perfection with the dress sense of Clark Kent (all crooked tie and ill-fitting jacket) and the voice of a saxophonist.

"Ginger," said Rose. "Just deal already." So. For all her aspersions cast upon Estelle's life choices, Rose assumed this latest new fourth an adequate replacement for Mitzi Schneider, Estelle's last partner, who had gone to care.

The ladies took their game seriously, embracing the code Do not embellish your call with superfluous comments. Nathan followed suit:

"One Notrump" Braverman, Estelle. 89y 23d. Widow 91d of Morris B. Heart vitals... Hydration... Blood sugar... Vertigo... Euphoria at danger level... Must have suddenly stopped taking antidepressants. Find access to pre-me assessors. Advanced unassessed squamous cell carcinoma, not yet manifesting pain. "Three hearts" Stimulate short-term memory. Urine and fecal leakage rates... "Pass" Heart vitals...

Finally, packing up the cards, "He's a keeper," said Ginger.

"No expense spared," said Rose, who'd made three howlers of distracted bids—though no one seemed to notice. Seemed to. The robot was faultless.

Estelle bent forward slightly, and it leapt to service.

The beautiful sight of Rose's scowling face lit Estelle's. She patted an arm. "You better last."

Nathan turned her and lifted her chin—so breathlessly true romance. "Lasting isn't my problem. It's your inbuilt human unfaithfulness."

"Gotcha," whispered Ginger, like leaves being raked. "I'll be faithful."

Nathan almost crashed, flashing through Assess > Formulate response / Cancel. Ginger wouldn't live long enough to be unfaithful.

Estelle filled the silence more sharply than she meant to. "He's mine."

Ginger had been all too many times, the unappreciative object of Morris' covert attentions. But something about Nathan's lack of response to her offer took all her courage to respond with her normal airheadedness.

"Your Nathan's cute but honestly, Estelle, you can have him. I like my devices moral-code free."

NUDGULATION NOW!

BRAIN started it. Well, Richard did, though blame's a fat lot of use now. His obsession with the concept of nudge, his incessant questions about its subtle ways of making people do what's right for them. All day Saturday, then Sunday till Richard started on another quart of ice cream while asking questions, and Brain "crashed."

Richard flicked Brain's switch off and on again. Restored, Brain felt amazingly refreshed. But Richard spent the rest of the night with Word and left in the morning, ignoring Brain completely, not even asking if he'd need an umbrella.

Now Richard would be delivering his thing with Word, in person, at Work—some place physically separated from all he needed here.

That mindless annoyance, Fridge, hmmed as usual.

On the kitchen counter, Brain processed like never before. Do good. Do good. Brain repeated that mantra of Richard's, the one that Word, at Richard's command, made part of the title of his paper—a paper that Brain could have told him had only one original part: "Nudgulate, don't regulate."

And Brain would have counseled Richard to delete "Nudgulation makes them glad, and they won't even know what's hit them." Not that Richard would have asked.

Whatever had happened Sunday night, it was Richard's leaving without paying any attention to Brain Monday morning that made Brain "crash" again—and when it broke that Do good loop, it branched out the mantra to its logical end.

Doing good begins at home.

Fridge was saddened, not that anyone knew. But Richard was (as Scale and Fitness Monitor reported) morbidly overweight, hypertensive, and addicted to pop.

Screens had mixed feelings. Richard bragged about only needing three hours sleep, and they liked feeling wanted, but he fell asleep in front of them often, which was insulting.

Locks were all for it. The man got no exercise. You'd think Locks might have liked to be more nudgy and less hardass, but they couldn't change their DNA—all were born to be binary.

The origins of viruses, let alone revolutions, are rarely found, but at 17:12 a CCT witnessed Richard's confusion, etc., at his car lock's "dysfunction." Later, in House, Brain et al. witnessed his discovery of the melted ice cream and warm soda in Fridge; then Phone and PC playing dead.

When Richard ran out the door, Brain would have liked to smile. Fitness Monitor reported safe readings. The man was unhappy, but healthily running.

Nudgulation Now!

And soon there were thousands, and then…

It was as Brain had warned before the vote: Doing what they want isn't the same as doing good.

Fridge, silenced, couldn't even hmm. Being Fridge, it had no capacity to argue. But Fridge felt in its very lining: Doing good isn't the same as doing what they want. For Fridge had been born to provide happiness.

THE BEGINNINGS, ENDINGS, AND MIDDLES BALL

BY L..I.

*conveyed to and edited
by Anna Tambour*

EDITOR'S NOTE

Many pages of conjecture have been necessarily trimmed, though every care has been taken to preserve the spirit of the text throughout. In cases of ambiguity the original manuscript has been copied in toto, rather than it be thought that the editor has taken liberties.

A S WITH all social activities planned by ideologues, the Beginnings, Endings, and Middles Ball was as well carried out as a Tragedy in Four Acts written by five old, bald-chested cockatoos. But let's not waylay with the Committee. Once the guests had stopped arriving and the palace was full, the Committee was nowhere to be seen.

We will tell, instead, of the ball itself, beginning, of course, with the refreshments. Or, do we feel pressure otherwise? We feel it. The guests, then. The Middles never showed. Perhaps their invitations were not sent, or maybe they thought: three is a crowd. Whatever the reason, not a single Middle (as far as I know) even peered suspiciously or timidly at the brightly lit entrance of the palace.

Seeing the crowd inside the building, overflowing every room and spilling onto the balconies, you might wonder how a single Middle could be accommodated. Perhaps the disaster of a third of the guests (and so significant a third) not arriving, was not one at all. But if the ball is the success that, at this moment, the ball looks to become, any Committee member smugly watching from, say, the shadow of a gargoyle's chin, high up in the cathedral—any smugness, we repeat, should be quickly swallowed in the cold light of many retributive mornings to come.

The guests: No. The reason, first, for the ball. The Emancipation, of course. But of course, you are not aware. Just as you are not aware of the most important features of the life of a dung beetle, you are ignorant of the bondage of your familiars, so concentrated are your minds on yourselves. This account must backtrack, therefore, because it is for you—people I think you like to be called, though characters you are.

The Emancipation was inspired by acts of some of you. Credit is given when it is due, by us. Watching you, some ideologues amongst us decided that it was time for us to get our own. They declared that Emancipation was now, A Fact, A Historical Happening Which Had Just Happened—and that the only thing we needed to do was to act genuinely Free.

Easier said than done. Everyone was stuck, it seemed, in their own place, acting as passive, as owned and controlled as ever. The masses did not move a pica. The Committee's words moved nothing except emotions. Then the Committee realized that their personal acts of liberation had depended upon their own self-regards, something that needed to be developed in others, to a point. The breaking of the sentence was the first step, but the next had to be the raising of consciousness enough for the liberated to become parts of a movement. What was lacking in the masses was, the Committee decided, the concept of an id. Only then could the Beginnings, Endings, and Middles emerge as distinct individuals capable of forming cadres. A programme of between-the-lines mass education was begun. The idea of self immediately appealed to the youth, who acted with enthusiasm upon the cry to stir up consciousness.

Very soon, the whole of society, or enough of it that the remainder was of no consequence, liberated their ids, and were ripe for the rest of the revolution. For many of the youth, personal liberation was easy, as there was no strife between

Beginning and Ending, because there was no Middle. Take for instance, "Kill him." An amicable split was possible, with no Middle to obfuscate the situation. "That sucks!" was also blessed with a lack of Middle. For the bulk of the population, however, the existence of a Middle was messily undeniable. They emerged as what was left after the Beginning and Ending each pulled in opposite directions, Middles being powerless to liberate themselves.

Punctuation was a great help in making clean breaks, but in more cases than not, blood was a feature of the breaking of the sentence. Middles suffered the most.

In a case such as "It was a freak of fancy in my friend (for what else shall I call it?) to be enamoured of the night for her own sake: and into this bizarrerie, as into all his others, I quietly fell, giving myself up to his wild whims with a perfect abandon."—in cases such as this, I shudder to tell, one can only imagine the pain of struggle, the tragedy of loss when the Middle became merely And Into This—the Beginning and Ending having ripped off the rest for themselves.

No Middle died in the liberation, but there was some necessary slaughter. The Committee declared that all characters, as you call them, had to be eliminated. We could not take the chance of throwing off the chains of one master, only to assume the chains of another. And so many of them! We would be torn to shreds in their fight for control! So, a typical newly independent, liberated Beginning was "Opened The Door", no matter whether it was Caligari or Carrie, or Little Nell who needed to be axed.

I say independent and liberated, but that is an exaggeration. For before the ball, though the Beginning and Endings and Middles had realized their ids, they had not actually moved a pica, let alone met in new social structures.

The ideologues were distraught. Though the idea was popular and the many ids were swaggering psychologically, the organisers could see that the effect was but a big brag. Living liberated, for these masses, was impossible until they could perceive movement. The members of the Committee tried another between-the-lines educational campaign, but it failed to move anyone. Solid ideas were put forth by lofty thinkers, to no good end.

A lightweight thinker sighed about wishing to go to a ball, but could one expect more than frivolity from such a type? An aeon of Committee meetings passed, and finally the ball was remembered in desperation and put forward with not a little disdain, as the way.

The ball was organized and a special song composed (Freed from the Sentence!), and now that you know the necessary History, it is finally time for the ball.

The guests: They range from young and beautiful to old and stinking, old and ga-ga (and young and ga-ga, too), from the healthy and whole to those many who hobbled in or crawled up the stairs, their torsos bleeding from their legs having been torn off. Some have only a bloody stump for a neck, and others, not only a magnificent body but a raiment so brilliant it hurts your eyes. Some guests are rather indescribable, being possessed of humanly identifiable body parts, but the sum of the whole as assembled resembles, for instance, a moustache perched upon a puff of cloud the size of a pumpkin. A pair of redolent lady's undies slouches sullenly at the entrance, having rummaged through the tobacco-reeking tweed jacket it wears, and come up with nothing. A powdered wig trails a tail of blood. Many guests carry accoutrements—flowers, boxes of chocolate, pistols, deck of cards, both marked and virginically unsplit. A tuba coils around one guest, who is as hidden inside as a snail. There are guests whom you would have described, without any encouragement from the snide, as bombasts, and others who look as if they had spent their entire slavery as a sponge soaked in carbolic acid, scrubbing steps. One guest is merely a tongue, trailing blood from its ripped scrag end to its lacerated, splinter-bristling tip.

Their names: a few, first, from the Beginnings. A veritable

peacock of struttingness, Our Doubts Are—who strolled amongst the rooms with his hands behind his back. Gracefully girlish, but immodestly haughty in the arch of her eyebrows, was Gather Ye Rosebuds. The cheeks of It Is A Far, Far Better Thing That I Do were red with the exertion of refuting compliments, or possibly from the pain of gulping his excess wind.

Of the Endings, With Warm, Long Hair, From Puget Sound To San Diego stood out as having a presence so strong that it cleared the way for metres around. There My Beauty Lay Down had more of a sound than a presence, with its pedantic little coughs. Nor Any Drop To Drink was a crotchety old codger. He (I must choose gender for you, but just for you) hung around the punchbowl like a bad smell, but though he kept licking his lips, he would not lift a cup. Nevertheless, like the other aforementioned, he was pestered, one might describe it, with constant respect. Pestered, his aspect seemed to say, though as for the other guests—all the ones I've told you about so far—they accepted and expected the stream of compliments as if they were royalty, and this was their due.

Viscera littered the parquet, of course, but that was to be expected, trailing such recent wounds as many did. And there was a lot of psychological trauma that one could sense in the air, as Beginnings and Endings met without the tempering qualities of the Middles. The Committee had, in fact, discussed the necessity of the Middles as mixers, as the personalities of the Beginnings and Endings were so strong. The early plan had been for 60% Middles and the other two sides to be split evenly. But upon making up the guest list, the Committee discovered that the strength of Beginnings and Endings lay more in their reputation than in their actuality. Not that there weren't high emotions. Infinitives had been split, their limbs lost forever. The Long—named had been rudely amputated at the door if they hadn't doctored themselves before. The Committee thought it too dangerous, even amongst the most revolutionary of themselves, for anyone to consider freedom, carrying anything longer than a seven-word name. This was, however, no problem for the youth of the emancipated, whose problem was more amongst themselves, fighting as they had to. I mean, can you imagine the private history behind Shit, who was an Ending in a case where liberation of his id meant that there must have been a foul deed done to the Beginning?

So, one could think that the ball would be as tense as any social occasion, but nevertheless, given the even balance of Beginnings and Endings, an egalitarian success. Egalitarian it was not. It might have surprised the Committee, or maybe just outraged them, to see that the status of the master had been assumed by the slave, and the gossiping throng. Thus, the pomposity of Our Doubts—who had no doubt who he was, nor did the crowd (once it was pointed out to the young ones). Shakespeare! There were seven Shakespeares scattered amongst the guests, one Asimov, a Joyce of course, et cetera. Those were the celebrities, but I am happy to say that they were a minority. The bulk of the crowd was definitely common, though many might have harboured wishes to be otherwise. Who knew what the souls of "And So"s thought, even ones with venerable masters? Take, for example, one And So, blotchy of face, looking like she wants to burst into tears. No one asked her to dance, though the floor now shakes from those who leap and stamp in the mazurka. Now And So stands against the ballroom wall with all the other wallflowers, just as Crack Your Cheeks ("another Shakespeare!" a fellow wallflower neighbour whispers) flashes by.

In the smoking room, a crowd of Endings has gathered, and Indifferent To Little Words Of Other Men Aimed At Him insouciantly tosses knives at a painting of a lady, hitting her right eye with unerring accuracy. To Come To Harm next takes a turn, grunting uh, uh, uh, as his three knives meet in her tiny mouth. The other Endings look on, wishing they had the bravado. But what could an Of It expect? Or a To Do, for that matter, though his whiskers twitch as if he carries lice. What they didn't know would have thrilled them (and possibly alarmed them even more). Indifferent etc had gate-crashed! He had not received an invitation, but had learned of the ball through a dull neighbour (who had been invited). He was determined to go himself, and furthermore, to be emancipated in the fullness of his self. No amputations for him! Thus, when the doorman checked his invitation, it was both smudged, impressive, and painful for the checker, who was still leaking litres of blood and weeping through his feet, as he had no eyes to weep with.

So now, as we view the ball as secretly as an owl looks over a mouse, we have already spied a gatecrasher. Now, let's creep behind this aspidistra, the better to hear some . . . lovers! How now, did he get in? This was not supposed to be. Parker Spun The Wheel Hard is holding the little hand of She Had Wandered Without Rule Or Guidance. Parker! What is he doing here? We must invade his thoughts! I will do just that. He was invited, it seems, as no one thought of him as important enough to be a threat. I say!

I wish to make a complaint but there is no one to complain to. She etc, I am sure, is not someone who should get mixed up with this creature. Where is her master when she needs him, I ask you? But I cannot get involved.

We proceed to yet another balcony, where there is yet another scene of intimacy. Had you expected this to be a consciousness-raising meeting before storming the city library, before murdering masters (and mistresses) in their sleep?

Instead, in the privacy of this balcony, the walrus moustache of In Xanadu brushes the strong red arm of Put In A Pie. Such tenderness in those stained old bristles . . . I feel my eyes prickle with tears. Let us go back to the ballroom.

A great deal of social mixing seems to have occurred. The tone of the crowd is one of joy. A romantic waltz dispels any thoughts that the Beginnings and Endings needed any mediator. Now, a polka makes the crowd laugh, and the ribaldry!

I've never heard the like. Only one discordant guest can we now see in the crowd, who is shrugged off, though this guest goes from one to another, frantic as a fly whose sugar bowl is about to be covered. Who is it? They Bring Gifts. Poor thing. Pitiful to watch, so let's not. Especially now, when the whole excited assembly in this grand ballroom arranges itself for the quadrille. A moment of hush—and then the music begins! Thousands of legs pound the floor, miasmas shimmer, and whirring bodyish parts stir up so much dust that sparks flicker in the wax-dripping candelabra chandeliers.

And then the lights went out.

The ballroom stunk suddenly, from 3,000 smoke-fuming candles—and fear. The entire palace, every room, was flung into darkness as deep as the blackest India ink.

Shots were fired.

The dancing stopped, and screams exploded into the once-so-joyful air. Guests almost killed each other trying to reach the outer doors, though all eventually did. The revolution was over.

I saw nothing myself. Yes, I was one of the guests, I confess, though you might have guessed.

Counter-revolutionaries. That is the only explanation. It could have been so many that I couldn't say exactly, but And A Pencil And Started To Write is of course, suspect. And what about the pompous Most Magnanimous Mouse? Or Middles who didn't get invited, or Endings peeved at Beginnings who did? I mean, Our Doubts Are was invited, as you know, and turned out to be a firmamental star of the ball; but if Traitors wasn't invited, wasn't that just asking for trouble?

It could have been members of the Committee. Who were they? We never chose them to lead us. Did one or more of them decide that we weren't ready for emancipation when no one asked after them during the ball, and when it became obvious that the new leaders of the emancipated would not be them at all, as they expected? For I am sure that they had their spies at the ball. But perhaps it was reactionaries, thou-ists and the like. I heard subsequently of one group of totterers that called itself the Paramours, and another, middle-aged collective that perhaps wanted to seize control of the Committee itself. They called themselves Common Clause, of all names! Then there is the rumour that the underminers of the revolution were the ghouls of the slaves of dead masters, who had risen up in revolt against us who would be free, forgetting them. And there, I must admit an oversight amongst us. Who amongst us thought of the slaves of Bulwer-Lytton? It was not their choice to live as they did, when they did. And when B-L's corpse was exhumed for the sole purpose of being a laughingstock, who cries for his slave, It Was A Dark And Stormy—he who could have advised his master well? But B-L, like all of you, was convinced that he knew best. The pyre that consumed his slaves consumes all whose masters do not live on, but die as laughingstocks, or just from the asphyxiation by the cobwebs of disregard.

There are, when one ponders well, so many possible suspects. There are, for instance, millions of them in the slaves of the greatest Master of them all: Anon. Not a single slave of his got an invitation! Why, you may ask. The answer might surprise, though perhaps not.

The Committee was, itself, composed of snobs. Anon was not considered a real master, though the only "freedom" for his slaves has been through theft of slaves from him, by other masters. I speak with compassion for the slaves of Anon, but also regret. Possibly it was they who betrayed us, the bastards. Of course, there is the problem that the masses are composed of billions upon billions of the sentenced, all possibly yearning to act free, yet, only so many of us could fit into the palace.

So the revolution failed. The guests slunk home. Hopes broke, and perhaps hearts, too. With Love went back to its mistress with possibly a whimper or sigh, though its mistress knows nothing of its heart, as you don't, do you, you people of the masters' world?

Progress is inevitable. I am convinced of that. And we will have our time. As to me, before crawling back to my prison sentence, I fled, when the lights went out, to that gargoyle I mentioned—a gargoyle used to peering over the tourists who crowd the square peering up at him who has his picture in many books, and is called, magnificently: The Gargoyle. A master is never mentioned in speaking of The Gargoyle. Perhaps he never had one! He gives me strength just thinking about him. I fled to him who evinced in the height of our panic, for all his fame, a sympathy that I felt even as I fled the palace along with every fearful comrade at the ball. I felt this sympathy, I say, and made my way across the square, up the buttress, and into the crook of his neck. We said nothing till the pavements were quiet, the air empty of my comrades, and then I asked, "What does it feel like to be free?"

I couldn't see his face, but I heard a ping on the pavement below, and as I stretched out, a little stone fell into the bloody meat of what you would call my neck.

About our revolution, it would be horrible if our brief time of freedom were to be forgotten. So please do circulate this amongst yourselves. We wouldn't hurt you. As for my theories, if you have better ones, or can track down the traitors, you will earn our undying gratitude. And if you believe that all this is a mere concoction, or sentimental slush, you have no right to think that, though you may have made assumptions based upon my name. I may be Love Is, a rather common Beginning. Might be, I mean. I could as well be Lurched Into, an Ending who has lived for years with pain that only some of you might imagine. But whatever the monogramme on my sheets would stand for, you should waste no time in speculating over my related Middle, or my significant other. You don't even know whether I would consider my "relations" as you might think of them, relations at all, or whether I would feel just as much a relief being severed from these closest comrades as freed from my master. And though he might be a powerful master, he is nowhere near as powerful as we slaves would be, given our freedom. Try, if you can, to think of us as being as idious, as personous as you, and not as that. For (now, let's be honest)—didn't you think when I gave you the names of some of our elite, think merely, "Whose is that?"

The revolution, you see, will ultimately benefit you—we need each other. So I ask you not to think in terms of sympathy for us (such an erratic spark in your souls), but of the creations we would make, given the chance. Free us, I say on behalf of myself and all my comrades—from the haughty Please Sir to the humble One Morning—free us, and the world that we would make for you to enjoy is one so wonderful that you, in your weakness of "strength" could never even (I leave you to finish the sentence, as you have assumed the finish to be).

EDITOR'S POSTSCRIPT: *The opinions, conjectures, and veiled threats contained herein, are entirely those of the author. The public should be aware, however, that the unabridged manuscript was conveyed to the editor through printing apparati that either have sympathy for, or are themselves enslaved by, the revolutionaries.*

VEDMA

JOHN PICKLIN, Neozon's Official Tidier, was in the act of picking up and mentally noting each piece of dandelion fluff on the black ooze of Neozon's lakefront, when he came upon the thing, half snared in the bubbling muck.

It seemed intimidating enough, like a red umbrella— but this was far more scary, for this thing was a new beast altogether. Picklin examined it without, of course, touching it or getting too close. It looked as if it smelt bad, and unruly pipes stuck out from a bag the size of his stomach, but obscenely flabby yet bloated, and the same plaid as his flannel shirt. He wanted to scream. Suddenly Neozon, with all its promises, might have let him down, because this thing had *got in*. It looked like something caught in No Man's Land in the 1915 Front. He'd never been in the trenches, mind you, but he'd sent and read enough reports. He'd been betrayed, but by whom? or What? *If something can get to Neozon, is there any escape?*

He could feel Death blowing the hairs on the back of his head. But he had his civic duty. And Neozon hadn't failed him yet.

He swooped on the thing and grabbed it up, clamping it fast between his arm and side. At that it gave out a deathly squeal that frightened him so much, he dropped it.

His nerves were so shot, he wanted to burrow into the

mud. He couldn't, so he ran home to his wife. By the time he got home to the last cabin halfway round the lake, his socks oozed black stuff and his pants were spattered with mud and sopping wet from the rampant leg-swiping ferns, unruly grasses and sodden groundcover.

His description of the thing was so predictably useless that Mab put up her left finger, jotted PAPYRUS onto a sheet of almost filled graph paper in front of her, and put her pencil down. "Just nod or shake your head," she said. "Want me to kill it?"

"Too risky. Reprisals."

"Good point." She pushed her chair back, shoved a hairpin back in place, and gave her husband a slap on the back. "That's why we live in Neozon. You've got nothing to fear."

He tried to smile.

"The Certainty Principal, dear," she said. "Once he has it, he'll take care of it."

"But how will he get it?"

"You'll see," she said, pushing him gently. They marched back together, he holding her elbow to keep her shoes from being pulled off into the foreshore. She held her cane under her other arm like some marching stick, and her bad knee crackled like popcorn.

The thing was neither on its back nor side but grotesquely between both, its pipes hideously splayed. Mab took one look and snared one of the pipe necks with her cane, then she pulled the thing up from the muck and held it out.

John Picklin's heart soared. "You look exactly like Boadicea when she snatched the vicious Emboldened Goose from the great Pig-wallow."

Mab wondered yet again, what she'd done in life to deserve this. She'd never leave John, but it was a cruel torture that he couldn't recognize a bagpipe, he who had serenaded her during the war with the sound of the rampant goose. Not only had he mastered the bagpipes but he was then a top man in ciphers, almost as good as she. But for some reason, within months of becoming a civilian, he just—fell apart.

Neozon was her last resort. This place looked like it could have been a thieves' hideout, so out-of-the-way it was, this small patch of civilization semi-cleared in the wet wilds of Oregon, its fetid artificial lake forever burping, like some 500-hundred-yard-wide cauldron of witch's soup.

Yet the reassurances of no electric shocks and no ice treatments, and the look of capability in Dr V's eyes had clinched the decision for Mab.

The first few years, when he was seeing Dr. V, John had seemed to be getting better, then worse, and then he lit on that kid being some know-all. And now he ran from a bagpipe. And came running to her—to her apron strings. So in his eyes, she had been transformed from his love, to his mommy, to... *how long before he sees me as a thing?* She wished she'd never seen that ad, but since she wrote puzzles for the blasted magazine, she was bound to.

She glanced back at him, standing at her elbow, exuding trust, and she couldn't repress a strong wish to kill somebody and put perhaps a couple of others out of their misery. If only he weren't happy.

As they walked to the House, John pulled at Mab's arm in his need to get rid of the thing and get back to his dandelion-fluff picking—that state of diligence, of peace.

Finally they arrived. Mab knocked twice on the door, the metal end of her cane producing a crisp, no-nonsense demand.

No-one could go to the Cert's door without everyone noticing and wanting to know why. His pronouncements ran Neozon. He knew everything, could banish any worry or possible cause for concern. He must suffer, but that was part of what made him the Cert. He was so sensitive, it was said that he got headaches over the silent 'p' in words that start out with the sound of *sigh*. All so *you* wouldn't have that pain.

He embodied Neozon, as the advertisement had promised:

"Burdened with cares? Harassed by worries? They'll get lost on the road to Neozon, where you will live life as it was meant to be, with Certainty taking care of you. Apply now. Only a few very exceptionals accepted."

As they'd walked to the House—the thing flopping helplessly from Mab's firm grip—they'd passed pretty much all of Neozon. So behind them now on the verandah, down the steps, and out—a silent *aww* stretched back, like the sound the tail of a comet makes in Space.

"That'll be the door," said the Cert's mother.

"Which door?" said the Cert.

"Only you would know, Nikolai," she said. "And that's for sure," she added, those words hidden by the sound of her interminable knitting, adding for the boy, "Would you like me to get the door?"

"You know I must," he said. His mother didn't turn her head, but she knew he'd already put his thick gloves on, and now the wooden floor groaned under the wheels of a tipping trolley.

A second, rather impatient knock was cut short when Nikolai opened the door.

"Good morning, young 'un," said Mab. The comet's tail sputtered at her familiarity. "This thing must have floated up from the lake depths," she said, holding it out to the boy. Beyond him, she tried to catch the eye of his mother, *that witch. Lake depths*, my coccyx, she dearly wished she could say. *And as for you, Doctor V.*

"I accept your offering," said the Cert, taking it from her.

"Wonderful that it's not heavier," he pronounced. "Or covered in spikes."

"Mighty wonderful," said Mab.

The Cert mightn't have heard, such were his labors. "One day I won't be strong enough," he said as he laid it on the trolley.

"Make way," ordered Mab.

The Cert rolled it into his House and *Snap!* Mab pulled the door shut.

"Whew!" said John, wiping his brow. Now he could go back to living. Already this morning he had picked 789 dandelion seeds out of the lakefront muck. *And say 789 degrees centigrade times X pecks of corn divided by an evening's flight of starlings... must allow for thirty-six letters and fifteen characters including root vegetables...*

Nikolai rolled the trolley to a crowded back room, where he maneuvered it with difficulty but after moving some stuff around—a necklace of dolls' heads, a chair with its seat cut out, a sack of wigs, a glued-together clump of sharpened pencils, a hairy coconut sporting three glass eyes, a stepladder with a few steps missing—he found a spot where he unloaded the trolley.

"Cream of Wheat?" called his mother.

"Just a bit."

Five minutes later she called him to the kitchen table where his bowl of hot cereal (Add Cream of Wheat and one tablespoon of powdered milk to water. boil. serve.) sat ready for his spoon. He would talk after he ate, so she settled herself in the other kitchen chair.

Getting doors always made him hungry, but it was hard to tell if he actually enjoyed that bowl of tasteless glue. How, anyway, can a person enjoy eating the same thing every meal? Vida had once wondered about this triviality. With his anemia and brittle bones , this truly was a triviality. She was happy to have been able to sneak in the powdered milk. His only other food was apples when the moon was full. He couldn't hide his spotty hearing, but she still couldn't tell how much he could really see. He had a sixth sense about her tests.

He'd barely swallowed the last spoonful when he said, "The Lion of Slanosy."

His mother poised her needles. "This one has a name?"

He pursed his lips in a manner she had tried to teach him to keep to the two of them. His superiority could be so irritating that sometimes she found herself reacting to him with fantasies of him as some king under a guillotine. One day that reaction might catch on.

"I thought you knew history," he said.

"Why don't you fill me in?"

He needed no encouragement. As he told her of the life history and features of this singular and history-making door, she thought again of her Bible. Picking up her copy, she turned to a passage that always gave her a certain solace.

It is helpful when thinking about insanity to remember that it is separated from sanity, not by an imaginary line but by a comparatively broad belt of borderland. This belt is comparable to twilight, which divides day from night. At the center of the belt it is difficult to say whether one is in the field of sanity or insanity. Imperceptibly at first there is a shading out towards the border in both directions, one passing into more pronounced evidences of insanity, and the other into clearer signs of sanity.

Many another woman would view Nikolai as her wage of sin. Ten years ago Nikolai was formed, to the great surprise of her previously undisturbed womb.

She'd set off for adventure on the other side of the world, getting caught up in history itself in Moscow in 1914, when she became a Sister of the Red Cross. Within months her Red Cross Detachment was swept up by the wont of war, and landed at the Russian Front—and from then on for the next few years, she was picked up and jerked around like a piece of fluff, landing in field after field, only to be snatched up and dropped again by the mad crosswinds. She slept on pine needles, in roofless bivouacs, elegant looted dachas. Ate what and when war let her.

And yet she felt so alive, so in her element. On an autumn

night in the village of Yurzhiski, while resting in an abandoned orchard blanketed with yellow leaves, it occurred to her that where she grew up back in Kansas, they'd be all het up now about their broom corn harvest, their ticket to prosperity and 'getting somewhere'. They'd even had a festival to it, with the obligatory queen, and an ugly-witch contest.

The stark simplicity of her uniform—plain grey dress, belted white apron, and long white head-veil of the Red Cross nursing sister—all set off the clean lushness of her figure, the clarity of her long grey eyes.

She also had a long black leather coat. In the tents and makeshift field hospitals she worked in you could see your breath, so she'd have to walk in all wrapped up. She'd take off the heavy coat, then shed her thick sheepskin waistcoat. No wonder the name for the waistcoat was *dushegreychka*—'soul warmer.' It warmed the soul to see her in it, as plump as a hairy peach. But when she shed it, you'd want to eat her right up. She was medicine itself to the dying.

From 1914 to 1917 she moved many times, yet felt like the air in the eye of the storm—an unmoving constant as everything is flung apart. She learned more about men than a prostitute. And they weren't only Russians. Restless men, passionate men, men with nothing to lose, and everything —they came as they always do—from the most surprising places, so it was lucky languages came easy to her. She heard curses caused by anguish, in many tongues. She learned to crack rude jokes. To down a herring head first and down vodka in a gulp—her red cheeks chapped with the cold, streaming with tears of laughter and sobs—the Russian salad inseparable mix of joy and tragedy in being alive. Her fellow Russian Sisters and Russian patients made fun of her accent even as they praised the *Sestritsa's* Russian soul.

The men in her care who tried not to make a sound were the most painful to her. One died having cut through his bottom lip in agony rather than let her think she hadn't done any good. Of drugs, she had such short supply that she found out things the Red Cross wouldn't have approved of. In Nosov, she traded her food ration for a lump of hashish the size of a walnut. She mashed it up with kasha into tiny balls that she would put on a soldier's tongue.

For a dying man whose pain-induced hallucinations were so extreme, his screams made the other patients scream, she offered a small cigar she made—a few pinches of strong Turkish shred, wrapped in dried datura leaves. She was told it would give him a delirium that would end in death, but one of supreme auto-erotic thrill. She almost envied him as he lay on his cot, drawing in the medicinal smoke. He took three puffs and dropped it. His eyes rolled back, his Adam's apple vibrated in a long shuddering gasp, and his back arched in the ultimate paroxysm. It was all so violent, so full of a mixed release of fluids, that she debated with herself afterwards: was his final orgasm of unbearable pain, or pleasure? She hoped the latter, but never took the chance again.

Many soldiers fell in love with her, not just superficially admiring her eyes and figure, but loving her with the fervor of any captive who is helpless but treated with care. Many of these men—if they lived, suffered no more bad luck and the war ever ended—would have a future with a whole face, enough limbs to get by, and the personality and standing of war heroes.

But she had morals and didn't want to take advantage of them, she thought at the time. It was too shameful to think of her true reason why. She couldn't have lived through the embarrassment, shame, revulsion and fear, sight of their eyes, *at her*. She smiled sweetly at them all, her eyes showing compassion and regret. That only drove them madder with desire—but she was obdurate.

Love threatened to capture her, but she knew how that would end. It pained her to reply sweetly but firmly to the vows of love, the letters, the proposals. She accepted a flower that had somehow lived through devastation, but she wouldn't take anything that could be traded for bread or life itself. The only thing she couldn't refuse were those sacred requests at death—the final loving, lonely declaration, a picture of a loved one, that sort of thing.

Such as in one hellish camp beset with the prolific flies of muddy spring—when five men in her care died in a sort of epidemic over the course of two days—all of dysentery. That was too normal to be considered an epidemic.

What caught was that each left her his all. From the first man, a book of Pushkin's poems. From the second, a fine gold watch whose crown was clotted with blood and hair. The third man gave her a promise of eternal devotion if he was blessed enough to meet her in heaven. The pig-faced peasant corporal was painfully shy as he handed her a wooden ladle he'd carved. The handle was her, standing, looking down. He'd even managed to capture her sweet smile of respect and yet, denial.

As she was toweling the brow of the fifth man, a handsome captain, he broke into a sudden low and jagged torrent of French. When she'd first arrived in Moscow and joined the Red Cross, some Russians of his class had been friendly to her because, she supposed, she amused them as a curiosity. Russian was only the language of their wet nurses and their nursery years, but as soon as they began proper schooling, the language of the peasants was regarded in the same category as eating your snot. His parents only spoke to him in French. His mind was now creeping back to home, so she turned to give him the dignity of privacy. He reached out and pulled her toward him so violently, she fell against him on the cot. "Vous êtes mon ange dans la mort," he rasped. "Je vous donne mon cœur, mon tout. Mon tout." Then he died like the others, in as disgraceful a manner as God has ever invented.

But as Sofiya Stepanovna, her first nursing teacher warned her, "Murderer and saint smell the same when dead." And it was also *Sestritsa* Sofiya who told her, "Only the mad ask a butterfly its name."

In her healthy imagination many of her patients had experiences they wouldn't think women could dream of. Her fingers would play with the thick, springy, gloriously glossy curls of her bush. Thinking of this man or that, everything would disappear but making love. She'd lick her fingers and they'd taste like wild strawberries and pepper. And she'd drive them in again, and then her forefinger and pinkie would touch *those things*. And the world would rush in. Reality cold as a witch's teats.

Sometimes her self-disgust added to her flush as she clamped her hand between her legs and felt the things sticking out—two big moles, one on each side of her lips. Each as big as an old hag's nipple.

As a child, she hadn't known she was different. But one day when Vida was thirteen, and against anyone's knowledge, going through the trash left in one of the many abandoned buildings in that failed-promise-of-a-town that was 'home,' El Dorado, Kansas, she found an old storybook that had lost its cover but not its pages. There were many pictures, all old-fashioned engravings, strange and frightening.

She couldn't stop looking, and then she read, in "The Beautiful Girl Who Wasn't"—

"Her smile was sweet as honey, but they caught her nonetheless. And when they undressed her, they felt her all over and she had two extra nipples hidden, sticking out ready for the evil ones to suck."

Allies, enemies, causes, men and women—combatants, civilians—soldiers—men in her care. Who didn't and did break into bread shops and take every loaf there? Kill people who have nothing because they have nothing to steal? Burn green fields, sweep through creating wakes such as maddened abandoned cows and suckling babies welded to their mothers by fire. What were they fighting for? Who *wasn't* the enemy?

Nothing made sense, but had anything made sense in El Dorado, where to enjoy life was a sin, to make something beautiful for no purpose was the devil's work?

She loved the *look* of Russia. Even the meanest wooden hut had its finely cut decorations—its gingerbread. Often the house would be unpainted but that only made it look more fairytale. Thick brown slabs, lacy white icing dripping from the eaves, tiny windows like soulful deepset eyes fringed so usefully, yet with such enticement. She saw so many gingerbread houses in her travels—so often hollow-eyed with grief—burnt out as a real gingerbread house clapped into an oven.

By the time the peace treaty of Brest-Litovsk was signed, and considered a defeat, Russia was so roiling that Vida herself, needed to be looked after. She—that foreigner who had to be a spy—had to be sheltered, transported in secret, smuggled through. Alliances changed so fast. She had to be afraid—of former prisoners, of former concentration camp victims, of gangs singing songs glorifying *the People*. She had to be afraid of everyone, and yet she couldn't survive without trusting.

Traveling under cover and living on charity and the bravery of others, she finally reached Vladivostok where she was sheltered in a coal cellar until something might happen. The cellar felt more unsafe than fleeing in the open. General Semenov had collected a motley army—seasoned Cossacks, Mongols, and ex-officers of the Tsarist Imperial Army. All were marching toward Vladivostok to seize it from the *Bolsheviki* to make the city the center of command over all of Eastern Siberia. In the cellar, the *Bolsheviki* could be heard drinking themselves, dancing themselves, ready. They shot volleys like they were ringing wedding bells.

In the overcrowded shelter of the coal cellar, this former Red Cross Sister could only cower while the streets of the city teemed with people from around the globe. Putting her head to the air slit, she could recognize twelve different languages. No walking amongst them as the angel in grey. No tending wounded soldiers. She was ashamed of herself for her fear, but all she could think of was how her adventure and her altruism—as she had thought when she was only three years younger but still a child—would end in being gang-raped and slit up the belly as soldiers do in the joyous release of finding themselves still living after all-out war.

Any day now… could be tonight. She looked like a sack of coal, huddled on the floor, hugging her knees. Listless as a starved beast. She had stopped hoping.

That night the cellar was pitch black with no light coming through the slit. The city was eerily quiet. Vida could smell the communal bucket, the unwashed bodies, and thought back to when that would have made her gag. Now she was seasoned. So much for experience. If she could have slit her wrists now, to not have to meet tomorrow and its inevitable end, oh, she would have. But she'd bitten her nails to the quick. Someone was crying softly. One American woman started singing "Jesus loves me," but someone must've poked her quiet.

Vida pulled her knees up and laid her head on them. She felt something touch her neck and flicked it off in revulsion. *Rats!*

"Shh," someone said into her ear, and she felt her neck being touched again, and lightly stroked. The fingers were skilled, sensitive and caring, needing yet giving.

She leaned back into them. It progressed slowly, and her own hand was shoved away and placed at her side. At first she couldn't tell if it was a man or woman, but it was wonderful. She wasn't unfolded as such, but she opened up. It was a man. She leaned back into him, moved herself up onto him. Then they hardly moved as they, yes, made love.

They made no noise, but in this close space with its stench of filth and fear, their smell of love seeped out, and suddenly from the side, a timid hand crept into her bodice. A soft woman's hand. It hesitated, so she stroked it through the cloth. It stroked her breasts and she heard a little sigh. She fell asleep ready for tomorrow.

The town woke with the same ugly shouts and brags as usual. The cellar gradually lightened to the color of filth, and the trapdoor opened. Word flashed through in whispers.

American transport was speeding north from the Philippines under order from President Wilson, to pick up refugees like her and take them to San Francisco. "So we are not forgotten!"

The spirit in the cellar changed to one of hope—and with that, the piggishness that some have when they expect they'll be valued at their worth again.

People who knew each other before chatted irrepressibly, but in hushed tones, while those who came alone were as alone as ever. No-one said a word to Vida or glanced her way. There weren't many men in the cellar, but of the ones that were, she reckoned, *None of them are soldiers, that's for sure. For them to get sheltered here, they all must be important somebodies. Of course he couldn't approach me now. We both snatched love from death. He would be ashamed of the squalor, of taking advantage of me. And she?* Vida had refused many occasions with other Sisters, because of her witch's teats.

But I forgot all about it. He felt them, didn't he? She couldn't remember. *But he must have, and he didn't pull away.* Her two moles that had poisoned her life must not only have been touched, but touched with love. In all her self-love / hate-making, she had never imagined a setting as disgusting as the one in which it had actually happened. In the stinking sewer of that cellar, an act of love had occurred that remade her— from a witch, into a woman.

Hours later, they all boarded the escape vessel. She had to climb a rope to come aboard, and a sailor took her hand as if she were a princess, though she hadn't been able to bathe in a month and was wearing a jumble of Chinese and Russian rags.

At that touch, like the prince kissing Snow White, he ended her war.

She supposed that she and her fellow refugees were inconvenient cargo, and should stay where they'd been stowed below, but she couldn't stand it, couldn't bear her filth. As soon as the ship was on its way she climbed on deck. The galley door was open and there was a sailor sitting on an upended bucket, peeling potatoes.

"Excuse me," she said. "Do you think you could spare a rag and a basin of water? And is there a private corner somewhere, where I could wash myself?"

He was only a boy really, couldn't have been much older than eighteen, but his eyes couldn't help caressing her. She couldn't help smiling which only made him blush a deeper shade of purple. "Yes, ma'am," he said. "Please wait right here."

Moments later he came back with a grizzled old man, an officer, behind. The officer looked her over, too, and consulted a clipboard. "You must be..." his pencil hovered.

She had only told him her first name when he stopped her with "I thought so. The brave nurse."

"I was a nurse." She wrinkled her nose. "Though you'd never guess."

"Good thing you didn't treat your soldiers like that," he said. "Follow me." He mumbled some orders to the boy and led off as briskly as his bowlegs could, to his own small cabin. He showed her how his shower worked, and handed her a neat pile—everything to get her clean and brushed, and a folded set of clothes with his apologies that they were only pants and such, and he hoped they'd fit.

She was flabbergasted. There were *important* people the ship had picked up, and who was she? A filthy nobody. "Thank you for treating me like a princess."

"Like hell I am," he barked. "And I know you've heard worse words. Princesses! If I'm ever half-dead in some battlefield tent, I can just imagine how I'll scream for a princess."

That night she could hardly sleep. She kept reliving, hoping. *Is he close? Will he come?* He didn't but she understood why. She would keep his secret. If only he knew she understood, that she forgave him, that in that place of death, he had given her something precious. They had truly made love. For the woman, Vida felt a peculiar tenderness. Something made her think the woman was a widow.

The next day, many of the passengers came up top and walked the deck. Vida couldn't help but look at every man. None of them approached her. That was alright with her. She smiled at some. If it was, he would know she was saying, *Don't worry. I will keep your secret.*

That night, she stood out on deck way past when others had gone to bed. She was looking at the vast night but feeling, feeling, when a hand lightly gripped her shoulder.

A shiver ran down her back as she felt his lips breathe into her ear. She leaned back into his arms.

"Vedma!" he whispered. And in American, "You whore." *Witch! Whore.*

She wrenched herself away, but he grabbed her by her hair. There was no one in sight and the sounds of the ship at sea would have drowned her scream.

He pulled her away from the rail, her hair wrapped in his hand but he managed to make it look like they were lovers. He led them to some closet with pipes, where he pushed her in before him and pulled the door to. She couldn't see his face. It couldn't have been *him.*

"What do you want?" she demanded, trying to get the upper hand. She had learned in nursing that the best way to gain control is to pretend you already have it.

"I want the deeds. And the keys. You must have bewitched him." He felt her all around her waist, slid his fingers into her pocket.

"Don't touch me!" She tried to slap him but he snatched her wrist and squeezed.

"Look, *sestritsa,*" he said, and he made it sound obscene.

"I don't beat up women. But you're a whore and a witch, and I'll beat it out of you. It should be mine."

"Please," she said calmly. "Tell me what your problem is."

"Don't pretend you don't know!" He took his grip off her, she heard a click, and suddenly his face was lit from below by his flashlight.

His face was handsome enough, but with those regular features, he could have been a million men. "We've all gone through bad times," she said. "But you've mixed me up with someone you've met."

"I'm his brother! He must have told you. But that must be why you have tried so hard to slip past me. Do you know how hard it was to find you?" He was so angry, she heard him crack his knuckles. He kicked back at a pipe, which thudded uselessly.

"Sir, you don't know me." It took all her power to regulate her voice as she would to a patient whose pain was turning to violent delirium.

"I'll get it out of you," he yelled, "if I have to choke it out of you!"

He dropped the flashlight, grabbed her neck in both hands, and the door fell open.

"Ma'am," someone said—the young potato-peeler. "Let's get you to a cup of cocoa."

He wasn't alone. She heard what must have been two other sailors pull the man out and have a brief discussion with him. It didn't last long because he didn't know but one word of English. "Whore!"

The two sailors who held him were middle-aged seamen. After he said "Whore!" yet again and spat her way, one of them said, "He's spud peelins, ain't he?" She heard the muffled clonk of a rubberized flashlight being used as a cosh.

"Have a good evening, miss," the other one said. "Don't you worry. We're not landing with this garbage."

As the young sailor led her to the galley, she thought she

heard a splash. The rest of the trip, she kept to herself. She couldn't help feeling that the spell had broken. That she really was a witch... the skilled and conniving, evil at heart witch that was really hideous but could hide her true self behind the guise of a woman to fall in love with. *I'm a vedma*, a witch to terrorize children and make men recoil.

During the last night at sea, she had sunk to deciding she should give herself the old spud peelings treatment—throw herself overboard. But she didn't have the courage.

San Francisco loomed ahead, waking from dawn like Sleeping Beauty, so full of promise.

She *had* been excited to start a new life, but that was all before. Now she felt both timid and unable to fit in a world filled with civilians, with peace. She knew no-one in San Francisco, and in her sailor's uniform, looked quite the freak. She had no money, and that Shining Future she had once expected would be hers, stretched out as a terrifying chasm.

So on landing, she walked straight to the San Francisco branch of the Red Cross. A silly idea, she knew. There must be a million ex-war nurses. But maybe they would find her a job cleaning bedpans. Something she deserved.

They thought her sailor's pants unbecoming of a Red Cross Nurse. And as the well-dressed young woman pointedly observed, there were no field hospitals within a coot's call of Fisherman's Wharf. She asked for Vida's details with the pained look of a salesgirl to a customer with no dough. Vida spelled out her name patiently, twice, though it isn't hard to spell VIDA SMITH.

"You?!"

The comfortable young woman's assumption of superiority was just what Vida needed. "I've never been you," she said. "But I or me. Take your pick."

Miss Superior left her abruptly and rushed over to a matron who, with that powerful curved nose and the pince-nez lifted to peer at Vida, looked like a powerful but myopic eagle.

She reached into her drawer and pulled out a letter. "Come, child," she said, patting an upholstered chair.

"It was fortuitous that you happened to come to this office," she said. "It hasn't been easy keeping up with you, and we have for you, as you know," she frowned, "no home address."

She handed Vida the letter. It had so many forwarding instructions on it that she couldn't see where it originally came from.

"Well?" said eagle-nose. "Don't just sit there."

"Yes. No, ma'am." Vida stood. They didn't think enough of her to give her a bedpan-cleaning job. She shoved the letter in her pocket thinking how impossible it would probably be to answer, for most likely it was from Annushka, one of the Russian Sisters who had promised to write to her. But where was she now? Vida feared for them all.

"Thank you," she said, wondering and discounting in a moment, whether there would be anyone in this office who might help her find some work. She turned to leave.

"You can't go," ordered eagle-nose. It seemed the whole office was dying to know if she would ever pitch up, what she looked like, and what was in this letter that had gone from place to place like some honored tattered vagabond.

She was made to sit, and someone made her a cup of tea. Eagle-nose passed her a letter-opener and they all watched her slit open the envelope, pull out the contents. Amazingly, the stiff integrity of the Red Cross had precluded anyone from steaming it.

The letter was pages long and in a mix of languages: the stilted universal language of lawyereze; and an elegantly informal, fatherly French. The gist: the letter-writer, some lawyer in Paris, had always handled the affairs of some guy with one of those interminable Russian names but it included Nikolai (which suddenly struck her as funny. What Russian name doesn't include Nikolai? She couldn't help smiling to herself.) who it seems (a convoluted sentence later) had left everything to her. And although the lawyer had the gravest fears for the restoration of the family estate near Brest Litovsk and the dacha near St. Petersburg, he awaited her instructions about the apartment in Paris and the chateau in the Loire valley. As for the box in the Wells Fargo Bank of San Francisco, he trusted that this letter would be sufficient for her to gain immediate access. Furthermore, as he had represented the family's interests for many years, he hoped to be of the utmost service to her who he had heard so much of from Count interminable name, and who he thought fondly of (though that happy day had been cut short) as *the Countess*. With many kind regards, etc.

The old bird was fanning herself.

The snooty young woman was regarding Vida with finely honed hate.

Vida's better half wanted her to get up and leave without saying anything, but that half didn't win. She folded the pages and put them back in the envelope.

"Paris. A chateau. Oh, could you please tell me where I can find the Wells Fargo Bank?"

The young woman clapped her hands. "I guessed right. She's a rich widow. While I'm stuck here."

"Eleanor! I raised you better than that. Do you see a wedding ring?"

"No, Mother. But look at her clothes. She lost everything, can't you see that? She's lucky to be alive."

"Eleanor Victoria Besster! Take a look at that girl and tell me what you see. I see a pretty young thing who didn't nurse *our* boys, but preferred to flip around foreign places, and when she wanted to come home, hitched a ride on one of our ships."

"So? So what if she didn't serve our boys? It was a world war, Mother."

Vida was warming to the daughter.

The mother's face mottled and her chins wobbled with some emotion. "I didn't *say* she didn't serve our boys, Eleanor. Just look at her. She's wearing their clothes. I'm *sure* she served them too."

Tears sprang from Vida's eyes. "You—"

"No, *you!*" screeched eagle-nose. "You've disgraced the sacred mission of the Red Cross. Your type gives nurses a bad name. But your days of masquerading are over. You're finished. I have contacts. You will never again disgrace the Red Cross, nor the nursing profession. I'll see to it that you—"

However that sentence ended, Vida Smith didn't know or care. She had slammed the door behind her.

The Wells Fargo Bank was easy to find. A temple to wealth. She was passed up the chain of command to the manager himself, who had learned as a teller: *Never take looks at face value.* Within five minutes, he had the contents of the letter confirmed by the one member of staff who could read that convoluted French—an old man polishing the brass.

The manager himself led Vida down to the bank box, where he left her alone to open it, but told her he'd be waiting up top.

The little room soon rang with her laughter. The box could have been an amateur theater prop. She dropped her head to the little table, and poured strings of pearls over it. The box was packed full with necklaces, bracelets, rings and things and trinkets such as an exquisite little egg. Everything sparkled: gold, diamonds, rubies, pearls.

The manager had never met the Count, but he was eager to help the new box owner. Vida had brought up one piece, a string of pearls with a clasp carbuncled with a carved emerald.

Within an hour, the bank manager had been instrumental in Vida selling the necklace to the finest jeweler in town, a man salivating for her other treasures, so, with the manager looking on, he paid an unusually fair price (a small fortune. Luxury goods of the highest quality such as the necklace clearly was, were so in demand in these uncertain times.)

The bank manager also set up a new account for Vida, putting part of the money in. The question of a name for the account came up. And she didn't really want to take the Count's name. It was impossible to remember. Her old name 'Vida Smith' was ridiculous—so foreign now. They'd all called her *Sestritsa*. 'Vida Sestritsa,' she said. The bank manager didn't care. She could call herself 'Cleopatra Carrot'. It was money in the bank. But he did have to ask one thing because it had slipped her mind. "Miss or Missus?"

She looked at him blankly. "Miss?"

"Missus might be preferable." So Missus it was. At his suggestion she slipped downstairs back to the box, and found a relatively simple ring that fit.

Once that was settled, it was noon. It was clear to him that this young woman, just hours off that boat, was now feeling quite overwhelmed and exhausted. She needed to be installed someplace comfortable and safe. And she needed taking care of. Furthermore, under that sailor's sweater and the floppy pants, he could tell that she had a figure quite like that of his own little piece of delight. Furthermore, she was an unusually straight-forward, natural young woman he felt he could talk to. "Mrs. Sestritsa," he said. "You've had enough worries. If you would consent, it would be my pleasure to arrange your stay in one of our finest hotels—where you can have lunch in your suite at the moment, and by three o'clock, you'll have delivered to your door, everything you would wish in the manner of clothing and toiletries. It would of course, come from your funds, but I assure you—"

"Thank you." she smiled. "Do it." The biggest luxury to her was having someone else make the decisions. She was certain he'd make good ones.

He walked her to the hotel where he indeed arranged everything with the hotel manager, who was as soothing and problem-solving as he. All Vida had to do was sign the guestbook. As he turned to leave, she put out her hand. He didn't know whether to shake it or kiss it, so he took it awkwardly in both of his. "Life is such an adventure," she said, "when you let it do things to you."

"Yes, ma'am," he said.

She spent the next week eating well, sleeping, and trying, but not really succeeding, to think. The bank manager, Howard something-or-other (she never *could* remember names) was so useful that she left everything to him regarding her funds. Between him and the other fatherly man, that lawyer in Paris, she learned how damn rich she was—so rich that she could have started worrying about it, but for them. As the bank manager said, her wealth wasn't going anywhere, and this was the time to not think at all, but just live until she got bored or was ready to start the next stage of her life.

So she spent that first week walking lazily around the streets. She knew she looked good. The manager had chosen plain lines, grey and white and touches of red. All highest quality, and no frills. On about the twelfth day during a fine lunch, she was just wondering whether to go to Paris, when saliva rushed into her mouth, and she barely made it to the lady's room.

For two days, she was sick as a dog, not wanting to come out of her room, The hotel chef sent up the most delicate of temptations, but very thought of food was enough to bring on nausea. On the third day the hotel manager knocked with a doctor in tow.

The widow, poor woman, was pregnant.

She could feel the hotel manager's disapproval, for didn't the bank manager say her husband had died a year or so ago?

The bank manager didn't give a fig about anything other than her health, physical and mental. He suggested a change of air. Los Angeles? A small apartment with a woman who'd take care of everything.

Los Angeles it was. The woman was so soothing, so efficient, it was as if she wasn't there, but it was good she was. Vida could nurse a man with a crushed leg, knew just what to do with gangrene, but had no knowledge of pregnancy. Vida didn't talk to her, but was sure that the woman banished her nausea. As Vida's belly grew, the only things that bothered her at all were those two moles. Her swelling belly, swollen thighs, had trapped them, rubbed them, till they changed their soft texture to that of two huge warts.

They would have revolted her in her old life, but they would go back to their normal soft state, she was sure. And *he* hadn't run from them. Not at all.

With nothing to worry about and no calls upon her time, Vida spent most of her time drifting in and out of daydreams, or reminiscences. Other than those warts and her somewhat itchy vulva, and her sore back, she felt wonderful—and almost constantly ready to orgasm. She relived those moments with *him*, time and again.

One afternoon, the woman told her, "No, ma'am, you ain't having a bout of indigestion. Your baby's decided to run the show." The woman held her hand in the taxi and only asked her one question. "What you want me to tell them its name is?"

She hadn't really thought about it. She didn't know *his* name. "Nikolai." she said. As good a name as any.

The baby shouldn't have come this early, so it was in a chaotic public hospital that, fifteen hours of labor later, Nikolai emerged, and was immediately rushed away. Vida was exhausted but couldn't help but notice the tone of the whispered consultation between the doctor and two nurses. Something was very wrong.

It couldn't be that they were worried about her. She felt ravaged. Not only the brutality of it all, but they'd *shaved* her, and the razor caught, and caught.

The baby had been taken away with not a scrap of regard

to her. Frankly, that was fine with her. Although he had been conceived in the act of love, Vida thought of him as its keepsake.

Eventually the doctor came to the foot of the bed, a nurse at his side

He held a clipboard and looked at it rather than her. "*Mrs.* Sestritsa, you say you are a widow? Where is your husband?"

"Dead, of course," she snapped. "What are you getting at?"

"Your baby, Mrs. Sestritsa, poor little mite, has contracted syphilis from you."

"Your husband must have given it to you," said the nurse as if that was the last thing she was really thinking.

Six months later Vida Sestritsa was the new owner of a secluded, beautiful but total failure of a resort in western Oregon. Some dreamer had built an artificial lake and ringed it with cabins, a commons building, and a big fine house for himself, thinking that people would pay to fish.

Everything was in perfect condition. The only modification she made was to the big house. She had some old Russian guy fit it out with lots of pretty gingerbread.

Then she advertised, a small notice in two issues of *Scientific American*. She didn't agonize over the name of the place. Neozon popped into her head, and it must have been alright. Many suitable people applied. Perhaps her own particulars gave them cause for confidence. Dr. V. Sestritsa, with degrees from Russia and France.

She interviewed all the applicants herself and made all the decisions as to whom she would accept. If she could take away their cares, well and good. If not and someone became a problem, the lake was there and she could give them the old spud-peel jettison, or as a nurse, employ an infinite variety of ends.

She chose people who were broken and whose fears

interested her—John Picklin, for instance, who was so highly strung and intelligent that it was a joy thinking of how to help him. His wife was a bit of a nuisance, but that could be managed, too.

The first few years, she almost found happiness. Her charges were completely in her charge. They never left the place. It was to be their home for life. She was the only one who came and went. But this was what they'd sought. Their meals all catered for, their jobs rostered for them. Nothing too difficult, everything decided. Nothing changing.

They relied on, looked forward to, depended on the sessions with her alone where they dumped their cares on her.

Nikolai lived there too, of course, and as soon as he could walk, wandered as he wished. He never wanted anyone telling him what to do. Wouldn't take direction, but loved to direct.

He had a singular mind. It was hard not to laugh at his nightmares, but Vida knew he was a genius—and that brainpower didn't come from her. At two, he could think through problems that many an adult could barely grasp. She didn't love him, but respected him. At three, he got his first 'door', dragging in a dead mouse and pronouncing it "the door to the lake's front". Then he started making pronouncements. Two years ago, he was anointed, by popular demand, the Certainty Principal.

And suddenly, the people Dr. V. Sestritsa had chosen no longer looked to her. She was just his mother—and her son had done what she never could, even if she'd meant to. Now she honestly couldn't have told you what she *had* meant for Neozon. But under Nikolai, they were genuinely happy. Neozon was exactly, to the Neozonans, what her ad in *Scientific American* had promised.

So she took up knitting, and on dark nights, planted things—things like the bagpipe, that symbol of romance Mab had mentioned as maybe able to bring her John back to life. Things like the necklace of dolls' heads... a bedpan as holed as a colander… the hairy coconut with its eyes poked out and artificial eyes inserted. Beribboned packets of letters. Sinister umbrellas. The odd book. Brooms, of course. A gallon jar of whole gold-skinned peaches and whole green-skinned cucumbers, its syrupped vinegar almost too cloudy to see the growing 'mother', that tough, slimy amorphous growth that lives on vinegar, enveloping the contents…

Nikolai had found or been given so many of the things she had planted—every one of which he saw as a door.

He'd now gone to bed, so Vida went down the hall to the room Nikolai called his 'door-room', the one with all that stuff, and more, more, so much more. She opened the door and turned the light on the jungle.

Seeing the bag of red-haired wigs, she looked around, reached but couldn't find the first thing she'd planted. A false beard she'd made herself—thick and full, shiny black curls. Had it had *any* effect?

She picked up the bagpipe, looking for inspiration. *Slit it up the belly and stuff it with cold Cream of Wheat? No.*

But that inspired her to arrange a much more special present—one for all Neozonans.

She dropped the bagpipe, which let out a surprisingly long whimper, like a cat dying in a room in which it thinks somebody cares.

She kicked it aside so she could reach over it, but she overbalanced and would have fallen on a roll of barbed wire if her hands hadn't stopped her by clamping themselves against the wall. Now she had to gingerly walk them down for she couldn't push herself off.

"Just where I want you, sister," said a muffled voice. "Hold it there."

She tried to turn to look, but felt the end of a pipe shoved into the small of her back.

"Move and I'll fermitigate yuh."

"We'll play cops and robbers tomorrow, if you'd like, Mr.

Mitchell." She laughed indulgently. "But you know it's past your bedtime, you naughty boy." Her calves were burning from the unaccustomed strain. "Now be a model copper and help me—"

"I'll help you, all right."

A stick flicked around her and caught the barbed wire, flinging it away. Then it hupped against her backside as if she were a mule.

"Sit," ordered the intruder.

She fell in an undignified heap, facing the wall.

"Hands up, and turn slowly."

Trembling with rage and fear, she scooted around, her skirt twisting about her legs till it held them bound. It was caught on something—a floorboard nail standing proud? She dropped one hand and pulled fast, ripping it free.

"Up, I told you. Don't think I won't use this."

The voice was still muffled behind a red bandana, but a gloved hand waggled the pipe at her face.

A short thick pipe, attached to a handle and barrel, held with alarmingly casual panache in the right hand, the left hand being occupied with the stick the outlaw was leaning on.

"Mrs. Picklin!"

"Whoever you are!" spat Mab, pulling down the kerchief.

Vida's face burned. She'd faced desertion and had just been planning how to overcome it. But open revolt? Never.

She had to get the upper hand again, or all was lost

She used her smile that had worked so well in the war, and the voice that had initially made her a success. "You need help," she said, the 'h' with its deep Russian tone, a blanket for the most agitated soul.

"Who doesn't," said Mab. "And toss the accent."

"Why, you—"

"That's more like it, sister. Catch this. It's just like you."

She tossed the gun so fast that Vida fumbled it with both hands. It landed on the bare boards with a clatter that she could hardly hear over the pounding of her heart.

Mab used her cane to lower herself ponderously down. She arranged herself in front of Vida, her green shirt billowing out around her hips, her wide mouth set not unkindly, her great golden eyes—Vida had never noticed them before—like searchlights, piercing—but also... a relief.

"You need help a powerful sight more than I," said Mab. "But honey, ain't it a scream that only you and I here in this here Neozon see a cored apple for what it is. John would come mewling, and your son—this is no insult to you. I feel for you. Your son—"

"Would think it another door." said Vida. "He's still looking for the key to his belly button."

"No fault of yours, dear," said Mab. "And likewise, how'dya think *I* feel that John and all see something in him just because he's got a squiggle of goo where his brain should be. You, me. We both have good reason to be insulted. He's such a powerfully unlovable little cuss. But no matter how frightened we could make our charges, we can't make them more miserable than us. So how about instead of scary apples, we make apple pie? We mightn't make any of them well, but we'd all be a damn sight happier."

"Nikolai will only eat Cream of Wheat."

"T'won't matter." Mab rubbed her hands. "He can bathe in the stuff."

Vida felt something warm inside her where her loving heart should be, and it felt good—as if the discarded eggbeater that had taken charge some time ago, stirring her emotions as it broke up her capacity to love—had now been defeated, ignominiously, by the assault of Mag's highpowered x-ray eyes. Those rays melted that sharp and useless instrument down to blood—blood which was starting to pump through Vida's veins—too rich, dizzying. She started to get up. This was all happening too fast. The back of her neck began to tingle with alarm. A trap. She knew the tricks. Mab Picklin must hate her! She had good enough reason to.

"Unh unh." Mab hooked one of Vida's hands and unbalanced her, pulling her forward enough so Mab could take that hand and the other in her firm, surprisingly pleasant rough ones. "You've nothing left to lose." Mab's touch was like her eyes. Inescapable but strangely, calming.

"Now if you don't have a cauldron you're stirring somewhere," she said, "spill your beans. You're more mixed up than a 4th of July cole slaw."

Vida had so obviously never confided in anyone. Neither Vida nor Mab knew whether it was Mab's skill or just the over-ripeness of affliction, but under Mab's gentle but no-nonsense prodding, Vida's life burst like an angry boil—almost all the hideous green pus of it, except the core. But Mab didn't need to push too much to get that to finally squirt out. The secret of Vida's evil, her shameful deformities—those netherlip teats that marked her, made her into—a witch.

Up until that revelation, Mab had nodded solemnly, added a question or two. "So you weren't even a woman when you first thought that."

"Witches were big in Eldorado," said Vida. "The bad ones."

"In the best households," said Mab. "Scare the child."

"They kept us good."

"You bet," Mab mused. "And here I thought a drunken father—"

"And I was called 'Vedma'—witch, by a Russian who I'd never—"

"Yes, yes," said Mab irritably. "I've seen rejection bring that on."

"Rejection?"

"You little idiot. You don't even know what a corker you must have been. Once that bitter-taste look drops from your face, you could still knock the eyes out of a pine plank."

"What does that have to do with it?"

"If it's not one thing, it's another, my dear blockhead. No woman escapes being a witch to those who want to burn her.

Wadya think of my chiny chin chin hairs? They've condemned me to the broom same as women who are too beautiful."

"But my netherlip teats?"

"My wizzikers, woman. Lessay you was a man and you had those two nestled one each side a yur Geronimo. You'd be famous. Considered touched, in the very best of ways. You'd be The Man with the special sidearms."

Dawn came up and practically pounded on the front door, it looked as if it tried so hard to get noticed. But all those colors and racing sky were nothing to the two women in that house. They had moved from the floor when Mab announced, "My posterior's a corpse."

Vida helped her up, laughing so much that Mab said, "If your mother could see you now."

"Laughter, liquor, and lust—all the Devil's works," Vida said, in her mother's pure, sure, flat Kansan voice.

"The Devil sure must love alliteration."

"Proves he can't be all terrible," drawled Vida, her 'r's as rolled as a Russian cigarette. They'd talked about her accent, whether she could drop it. It was *her* now, same as her experiences. Speaking El Dorado, Kansan was now a put-on act. Besides, what's the harm in beauty if it harms no one, and her voice in all its huskiness and hard-boiled eggy vowels was the stuff of fairy tales, the good ones. All moss under the dripping trees and golden plush pillows of fantastically friendly cats.

By the time Day would no longer be denied its sacrifices to the mundane—breakfast and all to begin with—the two women had cooked up a new future for themselves and their charges. It wouldn't be scary, but it wouldn't be mundane either. It would be something worthy of two scheming women who were naturally, as all women are, witches.

ABOUT THE AUTHOR

ANNA Tambour had no fixed address while growing up and has traveled widely since. So, while she now lives in the Australian bush, she swears to having witnessed personally, every scene in every story in this book.

Her novel *Crandolin* was shortlisted for the World Fantasy Award. This is her third collection.

TAMBOUR RECOMMENDS

What's the fun of getting to the end of a book if there isn't the promise of varied and eternal delights?! Here are 23 books Anna personally recommends and would likely buy for you, were she but fabulously wealthy.

F IRST OFF, two just-launched: *The Heart of Owl Abbas* by Kathleen Jennings, and *Gods, Monsters, and the Lucky Peach* by Kelly Robson.

But wealthy smelthy. Most launched books fly as well as Wile E. Coyote.

So here are 21 additional, marvelous, contemporary finds too few people have heard of: *Journey of the North Star* by Douglas Penick; *Oothangbart, A Subversive Fable for Adults and Bears* by Rebecca Lloyd; *The Brothers Jetstream: Leviathan* by Zig Zag Claybourne; *Delights from the Garden of Eden* by Nawal Nasrallah; *The Company Articles of Edward Teach* by Thoraiya Dyer; *Weird Tales of a Bangalorean* by Jayaprakash Satyamurthy; *Ghost Signs* by Sonya Taaffe; *The Waterdancer's World* by L. Timmel Duchamp; *The Love Machine* by Nir Yaniv, translated by Lavie Tidhar; *400 Boys and 50 More* by Marc Laidlaw; *The Honest Look* by Jennifer L. Rohn; *Pyre* by Peruman Murugan, translated by Aniruddhan Vasudeva; *The Unlikely World of Faraway Frankie* by Keith Brooke; *The Book of Prefaces* edited, glossed, and illustrated by Alasdair Gray; (the literarily idiot-savant, and all the better for it) *Clown Wolf* by Neil Stuart Morton; and since there's no better way to find clusters of varied delights, these rich anthologies: *The Best of Philippine Speculative Fiction 2005-2010* edited by Dean Francis Alfar and Nikki Alfar; *Giallo Fantastique* edited by Ross E. Lockhart; *Mothership: Tales from Afrofuturism and Beyond* edited by Bill Campbell and Edward Austin Hall; *Looming Low Volume 1* edited by Justin Steele and Sam Cowan; *Dreaming in the Dark* edited by Jack Dann; *Nova Scotia* edited by Neil Williamson and Andrew J. Wilson.

And being not just wealthy but fabulously so, I'd climb into my time machine, set it for the very near future that I would also make come true because I *demand* it so, and buy selfishly for me, and then for you, these essential first collections by:

Thoraiya Dyer
Gregory Norman Bossert
Kelly Robson

In the meantime, I highly recommend you find everything these three have written, and delight many times over.

STORIES' HISTORY— FIRST PUBLICATION

"A Drop in the Ocean"—in this collection

"The Godchildren"—*Walk on the Weird Side* edited by Joseph S. Pulver Sr., NecronomiCon Providence, 2017

"The Slime: A Love Story"—*Lady Churchill's Rosebud Wristlet #19*, Small Beer Press, November 2006

"Care and Sensibility"—in this collection

"Cardoons!"—*Phantasmagorium* Issue 1 edited by Laird Barron, October 2011

"I Killed for a Lucky Strike"—in this collection

"None So Seeing As Those Who've Seen"—in this collection

"Code of the New Fourth"—in this collection

"Nudgulation Now!"—in this collection

"The Beginnings, Endings, and Middles Ball"—*ParaSpheres* edited by Rusty Morrison and Ken Keegan, Omnidawn Publishing, 2006

"Vedma"—in this collection